PIRATES OF MARAUDA

Book 2:
RENDEZVOUS

by

FOREST FOX

Cover Art by

Eli D'Elia

FOREST FOX PRESS

Edited by Paul Weisser, PhD
Berkeley, California

Published by Forest Fox Press
Post Office Box 5694
Vallejo, CA 94591

info@forestfoxpress.com
www.forestfoxpress.com

Any similarity to reality is purely intentional.

This book is dedicated with fond respect and appreciation to all who helped me, too many to list here. You know who you are.

Preface

Dr. David Abblett
Clinical Report
Subject: Elias Kazmir

Subject's brother, Zoroaster, is my patient seeking relief from new onset phobia, which made him unable to continue diving in their family business. Under hypnosis, Zoroaster related a fantastic chain of events, of which he had no conscious recollection afterward. In an effort to get to the source of this problem, Elias also submitted to hypnosis and, over a series of sessions, gave a nearly identical account of the same events, which is recorded here verbatim. Like his brother, he had no conscious recollection of any of the events in this account that took place after they discovered and took pictures of a saucer-type craft lying in two hundred feet of water on the edge of an abyss off the coast of Bermuda. I have scheduled the next session with both brothers to present them with these findings.

I

"What are you telling us?" Dad asked. "That we all went off somewhere to some island with dinosaurs and pirates and Adam and Eve? Doc, surely you have to take a breath and think for a moment of what you're saying! It doesn't put you in a very stable light."

Dad's first reaction to the identical stories that Zoe and Eli had each related under hypnosis to Dr. Abblett was that the good doctor was being absurd.

Unphased by this, the doctor continued: "I know it's hard to believe, but you have these photos you took of the saucer. How do *you* explain it? These pictures and the fact that each of your accounts is identical lead me to conclude that either you suffered from mass hallucinations, which I don't believe possible, or that you did, in fact, go to that island. No, I've thought long and hard about it and, although it's baffling, it cannot be dismissed. I would like to send what we have to my brother at the Oceanographic Institute in Washington. Maybe he can shed some light on your experience."

"This was the third comprehensive scan, Captain. There is absolutely no trace of pursuit since we came through the asteroid belt. We lost them."

Commander Zalcon's tone was one of great relief. They had outrun their relentless pursuers at last, after being in space for a time that seemed endless. As the infamous starship *Maraudor* streaked across the Universe at maximum speed, her vast holds were less than a fraction full. Trying to outrun a posse from the Illuminosity took every moment of consciousness and ounce of cunning that the space pirates had. The Maraudians had been able to penetrate the pursuit tactics code of the tireless robots. Using a special program designed by their own ingenious hackers, they planned their escape route based on anticipations of their pursuers' every move. Finally, halfway across the known Universe, they had managed to lose the relentless posse.

The Maraudians had never traveled this far into the endless night of space. Onboard the cosmic pirate ship, the interior lights gave everything an icy blue glow, which served to enhance the Maraudians' enchantment with their life in space. The first relief from the strain of the chase came as the massive engines' ceaseless whine sank below audible levels. The solar waves dissipated as the treasure-class star cruiser slowed to impulse speed.

Captain Terran ordered, "Slow ahead!" while he and his staff considered their situation.

A wave of space phobia, a feeling like being trapped in a bottle, flashed through the commander of the *Maraudor*, a sure sign that he had been wearing the same clothes too long. The others were in much the same shape. Finally, after weeks of pursuit, these second-string priorities could be addressed.

Terran smiled. Framed in jet-black hair and full beard, his high cheekbones, green eyes, and long slender nose gave him the appearance of a Persian prince. A very capable commander, he rarely smiled. Although he thoroughly enjoyed his work and conducted it with the mastery of a pro, he always demonstrated a serious, alert, and motivated attitude toward the business at hand. First and foremost, Terran was an interstellar pirate. Contrary to the earthly definition, this lofty title spoke of a lengthy education, among other attainments, in all the related studies of space travel. He was the youngest on his planet nation ever to be awarded the symbolic keys to the Universe and the rights and title of a Maraudian Space Pirate. The Pirates of Marauda were exclusively chosen from the elite upper crust of Maraudian culture.

In all, there were fewer than five hundred such pirate captains commanding space galleons and cruisers in all the known galaxies. They were sworn to return whenever their holds were full, to deposit half of everything with the Marauda Funding Company. Also known as the Great Holds of Marauda, the ominous company was accepted by all, but only spoken about in whispers. This right to plunder, known as the Game of Kings, was played with a fervor that was genetic in origin.

Only a successful swindle was capable of causing Terran to smile, and on those rare occasions when the victim was the Illuminosity, the crew got to see their six-foot commander walk with a bounce in his step.

The Illuminosity, a robot empire, had maintained and controlled the countless peopled planets of the Qwarzarian galaxy for as long as anyone could remember. Their great web of industrial and retail commerce held the populations in a state of pacified contentedness that allowed the Illuminosity to harvest the intelligence of all their experiences. Gathering intelligence was the prime directive of the Empire, a dictum set forth by the ancient algorithms, which, like the robots themselves, had outlived their human creators. The second priority of the Illuminosity was an insatiable quest for gold. Only the rare yellow metal could be turned into repellite, a marvelous alloy, virtually indestructible, that was used to construct starships as well as the bodies of the robots.

Terran had his own suspicions about why his home planet, Marauda, went unmolested by the ominous Empire. However, such thoughts, theories, and speculations were considered taboo, and never openly discussed.

Among the fruits of the Illuminosity's harvest was the vast array of tools and technologies they had developed to fascinate and captivate humans. Terran had just stolen a prototype of another one of these wondrous tools. It would be a while before the space pirates figured out how to operate this latest prize, but

Terran felt confident that his profit from the mysterious device would more than compensate for the trouble the crew had endured to obtain it. Called a time portal, it was supposed to allow a traveler to isolate any moment in a given temporal zone.

"Time portal, indeed!" said Commander Zalcon. "What are we going to do with such a thing? Do we have the slightest idea of how it works, Captain?"

"No," said Terran, "at least not yet. We did obtain some information pertaining to operating procedure, and as soon as we can translate the robots' binary code, we will have to rely on Mandoon to make it work for us. Once we learn its secrets, we will have the greatest tool ever to assist us in our quest for the riches of the Universe."

"I agree," Zalcon said, "that such an apparatus has that potential, but up until now it has cost us more gold than we have ever paid, not to mention that it has taken us farther out into the endless sea of space than we have ever ventured before."

"Yes, Commander," said Terran, beaming, "but think of it. This time portal will supposedly allow us to isolate any given moment in a temporal zone. We shall use history as our map and send our boarding parties out to loot the riches of the ages. With such a tool, we could fill the Great Holds of Marauda many times over!"

Zalcon listened without any further comment as he walked with Terran through the busy passageways while their starship crept through the Milky Way. Slightly shorter than Terran, Zalcon could have passed for the captain's son. He cut a fit and dashing image as the first mate. Terran depended on him for his sharp wit and strategic aptitude. They were on their way to the science lab to confer with their senior science officer. Zalcon could never get used to the eccentric Mandoon, who had a touch of the muddled magician about him. The maniacal tones in his voice and his occasional miscalculations did not instill confidence in his ability. On one occasion, Zalcon secretly used his priority clearance to check on Mandoon's qualifying documents, which, to his surprise, he found in abundance.

"Mandoon *claims* to have already figured out how to set the calculations for precise time placement," the captain said, rolling his eyes.

Zalcon understood his captain's skepticism. Terran had been unimpressed with Mandoon ever since his miscalculations nearly cost them the only treasure haul they had made on this, their furthest space jaunt ever.

They found Mandoon hunched over the device, tinkering. A perfect isosceles triangle, it stood on its own, seven feet at its highest point, with a smooth grey metallic surface of unidentifiable origin.

Sliding his hand over the sleek surface of their new prize, Terran said, "We'll need someone to try it out."

When the spindly space sorcerer rose from his normal hunched-over position, he was the tallest of the three senior officers. Although he was not underweight, his haggard and pasty white frame lacked any fat tissue. The lab's cold blue lighting gave his gaunt features a ghoulish tone. There was undeniably something disquieting about this quaint concoction of science and man.

Terran's words had startled Mandoon, but even as he spun around to answer the captain, he projected the ageless image of a wizard. "Yes, Captain, to be sure," he said. "However, I do hope it won't be *me*.... There's a problem.... It seems a traveler can expect to suffer some...shall we say, cerebral abrasion."

No one noticed the skeptical expression crossing Zalcon's face.

"We can't use any of our crew," Terran said, looking at his first mate for input.

Zalcon knew that look and responded smartly. "What we need," he said, "is an associate, someone who will agree to do the deed."

Terran smirked at the first officer's response.

As if to join in on the conversation, the intercom came alive: "Bridge to Terran! We have located a treasure planet in a nearby system—the third one from its star."

"Acknowledged, I'm on my way," Terran replied.

All three officers were delighted with this timely announcement. Zalcon noticed a wave of relief pass over the wizard's face as he heard the good news. A routine visit to a treasure planet would supply all their needs.

Smiling, Zalcon continued, "We should be able to find some natives to help us."

"Yes, Captain," cackled Mandoon, "someone to do the deed."

Things were going their way. Despite their tedious journey, everything was steadily falling into place.

Terran nodded to Mandoon. "Indeed, Commander," he said, "it looks like we can do no wrong." Then, turning to his first officer, he added, "Let's get to the bridge."

The Maraudians had a wide variety of implements to assist in their relentless search for gold and gems. The quest for treasure was their top priority, which they pursued without regard for harm suffered by anyone in their path. There was one thing in the Universe they valued above all else. Every Maraudian knew the stories of the legendary Esseen crystals of Lamoria, divine elements that seemed to turn up once every ten thousand years. Universally considered the ultimate wealth, these crystals afforded the powers of the gods to whoever possessed them. There were many versions of this belief, but every legend about the miraculous crystals agreed that unparalleled power came with possessing them.

The treasure planet that the starship had discovered was the Earth—in the year 1819. As they orbited the globe, the ship's scanners soon detected deposits of gold and treasure all over the area of the Atlantic and the Caribbean, as well as other places. Many of these fortunes were in transit on the numerous wind ships that sailed the planet's seven seas. These initial revelations showed promise that the Maraudians' daring journey would be worth its while. Potential like this always infused them with an unbridled eagerness to pursue the prize. Soon it would be business as usual for the interplanetary plunderers. After a few routine procedures, all would be ready to commence the harvest.

Not wishing to make their presence known until they had the big picture on the natives they had dropped in on, the space pirates would remain in orbit to compile a profile of life on this planet, including its dominating cultures, customs, styles, and dialects. They would also use this pause to bring the newly acquired time portal on line. Terran hoped to be able to use the device, a priceless treasure in itself, to access the treasures of the ages. To possess the time portal and not be able to use it was an unacceptable option to the space pirate. Confident that he would devise a plan once it came on line, he turned his focus to making the small treasure planet pay its contribution to the holds of the *Maraudor*.

After orbiting the planet many times, the Maraudians had profiles on every major pirate on Earth and had already started contacting some of them. With less than a dozen prominent pirates left in the world in 1819, the golden age of the buccaneers had all but come and gone. Terran now focused in on three ships that were working together, systematically looting nearly every treasure ship that sailed in the Caribbean and the Atlantic.

The commodore of the rapacious little fleet was Captain Rosario. Known as the Phantom, he was a clever buccaneer who earned the loyalty of his men because he knew how to slacken the reins and when to apply the curb. He was also generous and always fair when he dealt out justice or severity.

The Phantom's treasure trove as well as his crew's potential to be expendable time travelers made him a prime candidate for the Maraudians' ambitions. Terran's procedure was to appear in the sky over a candidate, presenting an invincible force for plunder, and thus coerce him to join forces and pillage together. Rosario would be next.

Rosario was known by his victims as the Phantom for his ability to strike out of nowhere, usually at sunrise, and then make off with all the gold and treasure. Thirty-four years old, he had been captain since he sailed into the exotic Montego Bay as a third mate on a merchant ship, and sailed back out as master of a brig of war, the *Tortuga Diablo*. Rosario's tale was one of amazing payback for a grave injustice suffered by his father at the hands of Jean Lafitte, the Corsair from Barataria. Those sailors who knew his story gravitated to Rosario. That was eleven years ago. The Phantom did not consider himself and his crew to be pirates. They were not bloodthirsty scoundrels, but rather collectors of unforgettable memories and mountains of gold and treasure.

Now he commanded a fleet of three brigs, which, in addition to his flagship, included the *Blue Dolphin* and the *Jewel*. The three ships had a combined crew of nearly three hundred sworn buccaneers, true to a man. In only eighteen weeks, they had filled the holds of their fleet with as many tons of gold and treasure, letting very little shipping slip by on the trade lanes of the two oceans. Now it was time to give it a rest and haul for their secret stash. There, on a remote island off Bermuda, in a dormant volcano, they had a treasure trove that could be counted among the most opulent ever assembled by buccaneers. The Phantom had faithfully saved half of everything that was acquired since they had begun, promising an equal share to each of his men so they could retire by the age of forty. It was his way of doing things that made his handpicked crew a cut above the rest when it came to loyalty and dedication.

The wind was contrary, only adding to the apprehension that had been building among Rosario's crew. Free of the battle stress and paranoia of normal day-to-day buccaneering, the cruise back home had, until now, always been a time of free-spirited days, with nights of jocularity and entertainment provided by black Zabor, the captain's multi-talented cabin boy, musician, and dancer.

But today, a heavy-hearted mood prevailed as they made their way out of their hunting grounds. All three crews had heard the reports about Jean Lafitte's intentions to put them out of commission. These threats from the "Terror of the Gulf" could not be taken lightly. Over the years, Rosario had steadily and with great success spirited more than his share of treasure ships from the long grasp of the King of Barataria. Although Rosario's treasure trove was greater than Lafitte's, his fleet was not. Getting caught by surprise in an open sea battle with Lafitte's armada would quickly end the Phantom's string of luck that was now in its eleventh year.

As the tiny island vanished from view, towering thunderheads were collecting over the volcano, transforming the distant horizon from vivid greys to pea green against its black, cone-shaped silhouette. Their latest haul safely hidden, and with several tons each of black lava rock neatly stowed away for ballast and optimum speed, the predator fleet was ready for action again.

Unknowingly, Rosario had led the orbiting space pirates to his hidden fortune. The Maraudians were delighted with this discovery. Terran decided he would leave it intact until the Earth-bound pirates had served their purpose and it was time to move on.

As Rosario's fleet put back out to sea, the high command were still undecided about how they would handle the increasing threats of Lafitte. Inspired by a new idea, Rosario summoned his captains. It was past midday by the time Captains Pizzo and Bruno gathered in the grand cabin of the flagship. The *Tortuga Diablo* rocked in unison with the *Blue Dolphin* and the *Jewel* on the open sea as the three captains conferred.

But their meeting was abruptly interrupted by the excited whoops and hollers of the crew. Everyone was pointing up in the sky as the commanders came out on deck.

The crew was a chorus of shrill anguish. "If that's a balloon," shrieked one of the sailors, "I've never seen the likes!"

Captain Pizzo, visibly startled, pinned himself against a bulkhead. Seeing Pizzo's surprise, Captain Bruno grasped his cutlass and looked skyward, his mouth dropping open in silent amazement.

These reactions registered instantly with Rosario as trouble. But there was ordinary trouble, and then there was *real* trouble. When Rosario saw what his men were looking at, his heart sank.

"What is it?" whispered Bruno.

"Nothing good!" Pizzo shot back, his face ashen.

He was shaken by the fact that a balloon was descending with complete control. The frightened crewmen were looking back and forth from the terrible surprise visitor to their captain, waiting for his orders.

"Steady, men, while we discover how to take this thing apart," Rosario said in that matter-of-fact tone, which always brought a sense of comfort and confidence to his crew.

Recomposing himself, Pizzo took his place beside the Phantom.

Following routine procedure, Terran's space barge appeared stationary, hovering high above the Phantom's flagship and her awestruck crew, who watched in silence as a large hemp basket descended slowly from the hovering craft. The aliens could have brought their massive ship to boarding level, for this was within their capability, but not in their plan. The hemp basket was a nice touch, giving the sailors a familiar focal point to grasp and be comfortable with.

"How can this be happening?" demanded Captain Pizzo. "Is it a balloon?" He strained to see. Something was different, but what it was he couldn't say. "I don't think so. No balloon I've ever seen moves like that!"

Most of the crew were familiar with hot air balloons and seemed to accept the hovering craft as some sort of variation of one, but Rosario knew in his gut that this was no balloon. Whatever it was, it had come uninvited.

The clear blue sky of the sun-drenched afternoon was changing to the same deep dark thunderheads Rosario and his crew had seen earlier hovering over their treasure trove. As the amber haze above the misty chop suddenly disappeared, Rosario sensed that this would be a day to remember. The scene was branded on the minds of captains and crew alike. As the basket dropped its last ten feet, they felt terribly inferior to whomever or whatever was descending upon them.

There were four occupants in the basket, dressed in deliberately familiar garb, including one who wore a flamboyant captain's hat. Whoever they were, Rosario did not want these intruders to see any signs of weakness among his crew.

Trembling in their shoes, with imaginations and superstitions running rampant, the men stood ready for an order from their captain.

"Steady, men!" he called. "Stay sharp while we see this thing through!"

As the visitors came alongside at poop deck level, their mate called out, "Our Captain Terran requests a parley with your good captain. Permission to come aboard, sir?"

Parley? Rosario thought, noting the ordinary guise of this extraordinary moment. *A reasonable request.*

Whoever they were, they spoke perfect English and, aside

from the fact that they were entering from above, they seemed quite commonplace.

Without hesitation, Rosario responded, "Come aboard!" He realized he had better hear what these people had to say. To his captains, he whispered, "If there's to be treachery, at least we'll have them close to us. Might be Lafitte's men, some new tactic." He threw this idea into the air, knowing it wasn't likely.

Captain Bruno didn't think so, either. "This is not the work of the Corsair," he said. He was thinking of the many reports about Lafitte's intentions and activities they had received from his extensive web of friends and informers throughout the region. "We never heard of *him* using a balloon...or whatever this thing is."

The boatswain, Will Knox, caught the first tether line of the strange boarding craft. Under Knox's supervision, the basket was quickly secured, and the four sailors from above came aboard, apparently unarmed. All this while, the crew remained silent as gathering whitecaps rocked the *Tortuga Diablo*. Knox escorted the visitors to the poop deck, with Lieutenant Zane preceding Captain Terran, and Commanders Mandoon and Zalcon following.

Their smooth entry into Rosario's world was no coincidence. The finesse with which they handled themselves spoke of the high standards Marauda demanded of all her space pirates. To the Maraudians, plundering was the sport of kings. They reveled in their occupation with an ardent fervor. Like master fly fishermen, they could "match the hatch," and delighted not only in acquiring the prize, but also in the swindle itself. Highly motivated, serious, and insatiable, Terran and Zalcon were typical of the types who focused on a life of unbridled plundering. The Pirates of Marauda were a unique brotherhood, made up of the most opulent of the pirate nation's elite. Their voracious appetite and drive were fueled by a genetic propensity for seeking treasure. Their pre-invasion reconnaissance had included an understanding of clothing styles. Indeed, Rosario's crew noticed nothing in their garb that seemed in any way out of the ordinary.

The Pirates of Marauda were known in their world as an ancient black market empire. They fed on the ubiquitous Illuminosity, a military and marketing complex that strove insatiably to dominate the vast consumer bazaars of their entire galaxy. The Qwarzarian galaxy was an expanse of space exponentially more populated than the Milky Way, with planet after planet of humanoid populations that were voraciously accumulating anything and everything, especially gold, to feed their appetites for all things shiny.

The Pirates of Marauda had established a long-standing reputation for the fabulous treasures they sold on the black market. With a similar rate of success, they had managed to obtain prototypes of many of the miraculous devices from the great research and development section of the Illuminosity. Among their latest implements were their present set of scanners, which enabled them to locate gold and other precious metals from orbit. Another stolen tool could read minds like a book. It allowed mental images, conscious or not, to be viewed in rapid succession. Their latest heist, however, the time portal, was not yet ready to make its contributions to the general fund.

The plan was for Mandoon to continue to unravel the mysteries of the temporal device while Captain Terran used the time to systematically accumulate all of the planet's gold and treasure. In addition, Terran planned to train an able-bodied force of expendable time travelers to do the work he was aspiring to. Now, as he stood face to face with the commodore and his captains, it was time to start making this trip pay.

"Allow me to introduce myself," the space pirate began. "My name is Captain Terran of the great ship *Maraudor*. These are my officers, Commanders Zalcon and Mandoon and Lieutenant Zane."

Maintaining a business-as-usual attitude, Rosario followed protocol and introduced himself and his officers.

Terran's staff had handled four such introductions in the last thirty-six hours alone. A master at manipulation, Terran now had four partnerships identical to the one he was about to propose to the Phantom. Of course, each Earthbound associate had no idea of the other arrangements. Even so, Rosario was more than skeptical.

"As you can see, Captain," Terran began after observing all the formalities, "our ocean is above the one you travel. We are not of your world. Let me be frank.... We are from beyond the stars, far away from this planet of yours. We know of many other worlds similar to this one. We are buccaneers like yourselves, always looking for gold and treasure. What we bring to this parley is the obvious advantage of an ally who can attack from above with a vastly superior weapon."

This opening address fell on Rosario and his men like chain shot as the images Terran described both appalled and astounded them. The ability to attack from above would indeed give them an insurmountable advantage—so long as it was never turned on them.

"We are here," Terran continued, "to propose a joint venture…, an alliance in which we could loot all the treasure we can hold. Of course, we would want half of everything. However, this should still give you much more than you could ever hope to obtain on your own. You know where the treasures of this planet are kept, and, together with our superior firepower, we can secure it all."

Unblinking, Captain Terran had laid out his proposal like so much bait.

As outrageous as it sounded, the revelation that they were from another world was received as matter-of-factly as it was divulged. Terran silently noted this aspect of the wily Rosario's countenance, which stood out in contrast to the reactions of the others of his ilk.

Rosario was no fool. He was sure the alien was leaving something out. What it was, he couldn't imagine, but he knew he wasn't going to like it.

I wonder why they chose me and not Lafitte or some other pirate for this alliance. I don't trust these pirates from another world, with their proposal of a fifty-fifty split.

He tried to read their faces, especially their eyes, but he couldn't get beyond the fact that they all looked as ordinary as dust. They seemed friendly enough, but there were too many unknowns, and he couldn't get past his strong premonition of trouble. Yet, he had no choice but to play along until he could figure a way to get out from under these pirates. If there were to be treachery, he still felt confident in his ability to come out on top.

As Captain Terran finished, Rosario asked with a smile, "Perhaps you could show us a demonstration of your superior firepower?"

"Indeed, we shall," said Terran. "At our earliest opportunity."

"I thank you for choosing us, Captain," said Rosario cunningly. "I'd be happy to embark on a joint venture with you. But first I'll need your assistance to eliminate my enemy..., the Corsair, Jean Lafitte. He has a thousand men in an armada he commands from Barataria, his kingdom by the sea. Lafitte's intent on destroying me because I deprived him of many treasure troves over the years."

Lafitte had a special contempt for Rosario, who, unlike him, plundered American ships. Although Lafitte was enamored of the Americans, this was a one-sided romance. After coming to Andrew Jackson's rescue in 1813, he was revered as a hero and pardoned for his sea crimes by President Madison. Now times had changed for the king of Barataria. Shunned by the new governor of Louisiana and an ungrateful country, the Corsair was on his own. By removing the Phantom's threat from the sea lanes, Lafitte would not only eliminate an old personal hindrance, but might also win himself the renewed favor of the governor as a friend and patriot.

"I agree to eliminate this Lafitte for you," said Terran. "But I suggest we confer again tomorrow about the strategies we'll need to defeat him."

Well versed in proper Earthly etiquette, Terran offered his hand, which Rosario accepted in agreement.

From all over the ship, the crew watched as the parley concluded and the Maraudians departed, their saucer climbing higher and higher until it was out of sight. When the frightened crew turned from this awesome spectacle and looked to their captains, they were calmed by the expression of confidence on Rosario's face. He passed the word to prepare the fleet to spend the night where it was.

The atmosphere changed again as the impending storm disappeared without a drop. A searing red sunset was the last of this day's exotic changes.

That night, Rosario and his captains conferred in the grand cabin aboard the *Tortuga Diablo*.

Captain Pizzo saw potential in Terran's proposition. "What have we got to lose?" he rationalized. "Besides, just when we need a little help, along come these *piratas del cielo*, claiming to end all our problems."

With mixed emotions, Rosario agreed. "This opportunity,"

he said, "should be taken advantage of."

"It couldn't have come along at a better time," said Captain Bruno. "This alliance will be just what we need for our problems with Lafitte."

Rosario took note of the matter-of-fact attitude of his men to such a preposterous set of circumstances. His voice took a softer tone as he explained his point of view.

"We had no choice," he said, "but to accept their offer. They seem intent on moving in. Until we know what we're up against, we'll throw in with 'em. We'll play out our part until the time comes when we can see our way out. Remember, mates, it's better to be at the devil's side than in his path."

The captain always chose a one-foot-in-front-of-the-other strategy when the unspoken truth was too disheartening to contemplate. They would all be doomed if the Maraudians turned on them, and they knew it.

The three captains were in agreement as the night settled its starry blanket over the voracious little fleet. Each captain conferred with his crew, bringing them up to speed with Rosario's plans for dealing with the strange new allies. Soon, the familiar sounds of slumbering ships, creaking and squeaking in the rippling waves, spoke of the gentle sea that rocked the Phantom's fleet on to another day.

The Maraudians had been orbiting the planet long enough to become familiar with the operations of both Rosario and Lafitte. Captain Terran chose Rosario over the Corsair because the latter trafficked in a wide variety of products and commodities, including slaves. Rosario's efforts were focused solely on gold and precious artifacts. Terran planned to keep Rosario engaged until Mandoon figured out how to use the time portal. Then he would use the Earthbound buccaneers as expendable time travelers, sending them off to retrieve the treasures of the ages before they were rendered useless derelicts. One thing was certain: before leaving the planet, Terran would have everything—including the treasure troves of *both* pirates.

The morning sun was well on the way to its sweltering zenith in the cloudless blue ether when Terran's space barge resumed its position above the *Tortuga Diablo*. Once again, the hemp basket delivered Terran and his entourage. After the usual formalities, Terran presented Rosario with a chart, which indicated the movements of three different merchant ships within a hundred-mile radius. Two were twelve hours apart and heading for San Juan.

"Although these two are disguised as cotton freighters," he said, "all three are in fact carrying gold bullion."

This was news to the Phantom. While remaining silent, he realized the aliens didn't need him to find their targets. Pizzo and Bruno also saw the contradiction. Giving each other the eye, they said nothing to indicate what they were thinking.

Terran had little regard for the threats of Jean Lafitte. He wanted to start looting immediately. "We'll deal with the Corsair wherever he may appear," he said, "and make short work of anything he sends against us."

Rosario nodded and smiled. Although he had not yet seen the superior firepower promised by Terran, he had seen the wondrous saucer craft and the manner in which these sky pirates were able to come and go. He would give them the benefit of the doubt for now, but their presence had awakened in him and his crew a gnawing in the pit of their stomachs, a nasty sensation that would not go away.

The first target was a merchantman of medium size, less than seventy miles to the southwest.

"An all-night cruise will put us in position by midday," said Rosario.

"According to my information," Terran said, "this merchantman is slow and has a wide turning radius. She's carrying fourteen to twenty cannons. She's also the closest target to your current position. My crew will not take part in the actual boarding. I need my people to remain at their stations."

"I see no problem," Rosario replied, "as long as the superior firepower you promise is readily available."

"If there are any unexpected developments," Terran concluded, "I will return with the news. Otherwise, we will rendezvous in twenty-four hours at the agreed target."

By the time Captains Pizzo and Bruno had returned to their respective commands, Rosario was already making sail with every stitch of canvas the great brig could manage. By early afternoon, all of his ships were under way with favorable winds.

According to Terran's map, there was no sign of the Corsair in the area. Nevertheless, keeping an eye out on the horizon, the Phantom still wondered if Terran would even know if the Corsair surprised them.

When the *Tortuga Diablo* arrived at the coordinates after an uneventful cruise, the lookout spotted the familiar silhouette of a merchantman on the horizon. She was rigged fore and aft with a mainsail and a square-rigged foremast. There was something protruding from her bow. The Phantom knew what it was, but said nothing, hoping he was wrong.

The merchantman's configuration gave her speed and some unique sailing abilities. Rosario knew these things spoke of a tough opponent. A skilled master could maneuver her with great elegance. Even so, the Phantom was confident he would soon overtake her.

There was no sign of the Maraudians as the fleet broke formation.

The wind shifted in Rosario's favor, causing the prize to make a broad reach. While the *Tortuga Diablo* continued straight for the target, the *Blue Dolphin* made for the forward approach. The *Jewel* sought to come from behind, leaving no effective route of escape.

The sun was past its zenith in the cloudless sapphire. The golden sunshine gave an amber glow to the fine saline mist kicked up by sporadic whitecaps.

Shortly after the Phantom's ships broke formation, the prize veered from the *Tortuga Diablo* and continued on a collision course with the *Blue Dolphin*. Rosario and Captain Bruno adjusted course and continued to close on their quarry. While her decks were being cleared for action, the gold runner was relentless as she bore down on the *Blue Dolphin*.

Two hours into the pursuit, there was still no sign of the allies from the sky as the *Blue Dolphin* came around on the target with all guns to bear. Things had become desperate. Captain Pizzo knew there wouldn't be time to reload for a second barrage as he angled the *Blue Dolphin* into position. He would only get one chance to stop a devastating collision, so he waited for his best shot.

They were close enough now to see her name — the *Fidelidad*. Her captain wasn't going down without a fight. Using every stitch of canvas she could manage, the *Fidelidad* would sell her life dearly if she couldn't get away. Unlike the other two merchant ships on Terran's chart, the *Fidelidad* made no attempt to disguise her true potential. Scudding along with the wind and steadily building to a devastating speed, she was equipped with a powerful battering ram on the bow, complete with a massive fist sculpted into its protrusion. The mere presence of such a device spoke of a severe attitude and determination to protect her precious cargo at all cost.

There was urgency in the wind. The afternoon trades transformed the restless surface into a contrary sea of whitecaps as each ship strove for her objective.

Undaunted, the guileful captain of the *Fidelidad* provided the smallest target possible to the pirates. Rosario had every sail pulling him to intercept, but that would not be enough. Realizing this, the Phantom came around for a broadside barrage as soon as he was in range. The *Tortuga Diablo* was hauling at maximum speed as she came into the wind and her sails quit, stabilizing the great flagship while the crew adjusted for the long shot and waited for the up roll. Rosario would have more to shoot at than the *Blue Dolphin* would. It was a desperate maneuver, but the only one that could possibly change the outcome of the battle.

In this situation, the *Fidelidad*'s maneuver was brilliant. By veering for the *Dolphin*, she eliminated the *Jewel*'s ability to come in for a quick response.

Captain Pizzo let loose with his best shot. Loaded with cannonballs chained together, his guns thundered almost in unison, and the rigging busters flew at the gold runner. The savvy captain of the *Fidelidad* anticipated the barrage, and once again his speeding ship veered to the port before resuming course at ramming speed. The evasive maneuver was that of a skilled master who knew how to avoid the majority of the specialized projectiles. Sustaining only minor damage, he would have the *Dolphin* in a few more minutes.

Rosario let fly his desperate long ball shots. The clipper was moving too fast even for the well-anticipated lead afforded by Rosario's guns. Narrowly missing the elusive skipper, the hurtling sable flock of destroyers fell away innocuously into the whitecaps. The *Fidelidad* ignored the flagship's barrage, her own cannons remaining silent as she continued to close on Captain Pizzo. There was no hope left for the *Blue Dolphin*. With less than two hundred yards until contact, everyone on both ships braced for the inevitable.

Suddenly, there was a piercing noise unlike anything they had ever heard before. Loud and high-pitched, it provided a concussive sensation, a swimming flash of dizziness that pounded the chest and caught the breath. This was repeated three times in rapid succession. In the midst of this shocking sensation, the crew was astonished to see the entire bow section and ramming device of the *Fidelidad* burst into a million splinters, and the great masts topple with sails torn and shredded.

Before anyone knew what had happened, the *Fidelidad* was dead in the water, with its front section flooding and its great spars broken and lying by her side. Her crewmen, some sitting, some sprawled about the deck, were stunned and befuddled.

Rosario was still closing and would be alongside the stricken merchantman within minutes. The commodore was the first to figure out what had happened. Looking up, he saw them, hovering as usual at a hundred feet. The crew cheered when they saw who it was that had saved the day for the *Blue Dolphin*. There was no fire or explosion, yet the gold runner was a total loss and would sink to the bottom within hours.

A large merchant ship, she was slower and had a wider turning radius than the *Tortuga Diablo*. With only sixteen cannons and a crew half the size of the Phantom's, the *Fidelidad*'s desperate action had made it clear that her captain had no intention of giving up his precious cargo. But in less than a minute, the tables had turned.

As Rosario came alongside, his men stood ready to loot the sinking derelict while there was still time. The boarding party went unhindered as they walked past the dazed sailors lying about. Never tipping their hand, the Phantom's crew did not let on how terrifying they found the marvelous weapon from the sky. Instead, they made light of the incapacitated crew of the *Fidelidad* as they went about their plunder.

"This is indeed a better way to come aboardin'," quipped one of Rosario's salts. "No fussin' or fightin', just help ourselves while these blokes sit and watch."

It turned into a warm, lazy afternoon. A soft breeze replaced the morning trades, and the sea was more green than blue as it rolled gently, with no evidence of the events that had just taken place. The Phantom's crew were in a state of false confidence.

They quickly located the bullion and offloaded four hundred and thirty-six bars. Before leaving the derelict, they put the survivors in longboats, knowing that the shaken crew would be discovered before too long on the busy sea lanes. This, too, was the mark of the Phantom, to show mercy after business was concluded. They were sailors of fortune, after all, not bloodthirsty pirates. They held no ill feeling for the opponent; they only wanted his prize.

As the ill-fated survivors bobbed about in their lifeboats, still senseless, they had no way of knowing how fortunate it was that Rosario led this mission. If Terran had been in command, they would soon be at the bottom, along with their ship.

As the Phantom sailed off toward San Juan and his rendezvous with the new allies, he directed his crew to divide the bullion into two equal piles on deck.

To his first mate, Rodriguez, he confided, "Although we did all the work, it wouldn't have been so easy if *they* hadn't supplied that superior firepower.... And now we're two hundred and eighteen bars of gold richer."

Rodriguez nodded as he considered his captain's words. It had been a year since that terrible night in the Grand Bahamas when the *Tortuga Diablo* was almost lost in a howling gale that swept four of her crew, including the previous first mate, from the decks. His twenty years of sea savvy and the fact that he had been with the Phantom from the beginning made it obvious to the crew why Rosario had chosen Rodriguez.

"Aye, Captain," he said, "it was a very close call. Another blink of the eyes, and we would've all been singing a different tune."

Rodriguez could always be relied on for his grounding version of reality.

Rosario nodded.

They sailed in silence to the rendezvous over the rolling main in what seemed to be only a few moments of contemplation, but was actually two hours.

As they watched the familiar basket lower away, Rosario and his men grew more apprehensive. Knowing that their new ally had such a heavy upper hand, they could not overlook the devastating potential of this tenuous alliance.

Rosario gave his captains last-minute instructions. "Whatever that weapon is," he said, "it will suffice for anything we need to do. We'll say no more about it."

The thrill of high adventure mixed with waves of terror ran through the sailors like hot and cold flashes as the sky pirates' gondola came onboard once again—this time with only Commander Zalcon and Lieutenant Zane.

Rosario watched them approach, musing that it might be lack of sea legs that gave Zalcon his arrogant swagger.

"I trust you are satisfied with our firepower," said Zalcon with not so subtle mockery.

With a fiery glare meant to check the commander's budding conceit, Rosario shot back, "I only hope that in the future you will be a little more gracious with your timing."

"All is well that ends well," Zalcon retorted, using the cliché to move on to the business at hand. "First of all, your men can offload our share while we talk."

Rosario noticed the Commander's unsettling tone, as if it were a storm cloud on the horizon.

I wonder if he's trying to tell me something.

To counterpoint Zalcon's blunt manner, Rosario casually pointed to the two piles of bullion gleaming on the weather deck. His phenomenal success as a buccaneer was due in no small part to his natural ability to read and lead men. It was this uncanny talent that now throbbed on his nerves, agitating a sense of command that had never before known uncertainty. After the Maraudians inspected and counted the four hundred and thirty-six bars, Knox and his men offloaded their half.

On the poop deck, Zalcon opened the chart on which they were tracking their quarries. Upon his first glance at this strange but accurate chart, Rodriguez flashed a troubled eye at his captain, which Rosario acknowledged with a single rise and fall of his thick eyebrow.

It became evident to Rosario's men that the information on the chart could only have been assembled from actual sightings. It showed the current positions of the two remaining gold runners closing on San Juan, one about ten hours behind the other. They were both at least twelve hours away.

"You will have to make sail immediately to be in position to intercept the first one at dawn," Zalcon said. "But don't worry, we will make short work of any situation that develops."

Pointing to the chart, Rosario replied, "Don't worry, says you? What about these four ships, each within fifty miles of our next prize?"

"They're just routine traffic," Lieutenant Zane said. "Nothing more."

"You don't find it suspicious that they're all pointed toward our quarry..., from four different directions?"

"Just be at these coordinates by dawn," Zane said coolly.

"Agreed," said Rosario, "but keep a sharp eye out on those four ships. I don't like the smell of it."

Zane nodded. "Unless there are new developments," he said, "we will see you at dawn at the rendezvous."

The meeting concluded as the late afternoon sun began to color the horizon, sending its amber glow across the sky. The heavily laden basket showed no strain from its precious cargo as it lifted off.

Rosario and his crew could not escape feeling inferior to these space pirates as they watched them go in this awesome manner, to say nothing of the strange and deadly weapon they possessed. The Phantom could not shrug off a deep sense of hopelessness about his inevitable fate with these superpirates.

What drives men to value gold and treasure above all else also binds them to a predictable treachery.

He knew the time would come when he would have to deal with their brand of betrayal. Even though their first mission together had been a success, his instinctive suspicions persisted, undermining his usual store of self-confidence. High morale was too valuable at sea to squander, and so he kept his pessimistic feelings to himself. So far, this new alliance had paid off, and that was the objective.

Once again, the *Tortuga Diablo* was under way as Captains Pizzo and Bruno were returning to their ships. The setting sun seared the faded blue sky with bands of red emanating from the sinking crimson cauldron. After the star's stunning last state-ment, the evening mantle settled into a moonless night. Only the aft lanterns revealed the fleet's presence as it sliced through the inky brine under full sail and high winds.

Rosario had outfitted his ships with the finest cotton sails, woven in India. The swiftness they afforded was instrumental in establishing the Phantom's reputation for speed and agility. Now they ensured his promptness as the fleet struck on through the night to the sunrise appointment.

Sleep was elusive for Rosario, whose mind was struggling to keep up with all that had happened. But mulling everything over always brought the same dismal conclusion: *We have no choice.*

Onboard the *Maraudor*, Captain Terran was considering Mandoon's latest report.

"When we activate the time portal," the science officer said, "I believe there will be a temporal signature known as a time spike."

"It's unsettling, Mandoon," said Terran with irritation, "that you failed to see this obstruction in the first place."

"Sir, the only ones with the technology and the inclination to police the temporal corridors are the Illuminosity…, but their ability to monitor anything at this distance is doubtful. Nevertheless, we have no way to be certain. At face value, this could be a substantial setback."

While it was true that the ominous empire had always left Terran's home planet unmolested, there were many occasions when Maraudian pirates had been marooned and their ships confiscated. In each instance, the captains in question had either failed or were too long overdue in making their contributions to the Great Holds of Marauda. Terran always paid well for good information. This was the key to his string of successful heists, which had yielded many of the tools developed by the empire's miraculous technology. He knew that there could be no doubt that a detected time spike would bring the empire's wrath down upon him.

Glaring at Mandoon, he said, "I'm sure, Commander, you will find a way around this latest obstacle. Until you do, however, we dare not activate the device." The soft, constant chirps and bleeps aboard the *Maraudor* were a sharp contrast to the low irascible tones of the terrible Terran. "We will be here a while before we can retrieve all this planet has to offer. I trust you will find the solutions we need to go forward by then."

Commander Zalcon stood silently while Terran laid out his expectations.

Mandoon tried to appear in control of the situation, but by doing so he presented a vision of false confidence. This escaped the irritated captain, but made Zalcon stifle a chuckle behind his hand. Terran's dissatisfaction never failed to trigger in Mandoon a bout with the claustrophobic state known as space sickness.

The space wizard tried to mask his nausea and anxiety with cool and calculated words. "I'm working on the problem day and night, Captain," he replied. "Hopefully, I will have some results for you before much longer."

This, too, Terran found unsettling. Gone was the maniacal undertone usually present in Mandoon's voice. Whenever he spoke in calm and collected tones, it was a sure sign of his uncertainty.

Terran and Zalcon nodded to each other in recognition of

this often discussed observation, a glance that Mandoon noticed as well. His fragile confidence was now collapsing. The very air was being sucked out of the compartment, or so it seemed.

"Bridge to Captain!"

Terran's focus shifted to the voice from the bridge. For Mandoon, the abrupt interruption was pure relief.

"What is it?"

"Captain, all four ships have altered course and appear to be attempting a rendezvous with the target."

"Very well, I'm on my way."

Terran gave Mandoon a last penetrating glare as he left the science deck with Zalcon.

On their way to the bridge, Terran muttered to his first mate, "I'm sure we will come up with a way to mask the time signature. The cerebral abrasions problem may not be so easy to solve."

They both knew very little about such things as temporal corridors and how these should be traveled. Choosing the time spike problem over the temporal abrasions as the easier one to overcome was purely arbitrary. This way of thinking was a device the Maraudians used to postulate a working premise, and ultimately acquire their prize. Trial and error was their method of mastering whatever skills were necessary to achieve success.

The space pirates had stolen the only prototype that existed. So far as they knew, the time portal might not have been perfected. The Illuminosity had been on a new frontier, with the time portal as its first attempt at temporal exploration. The research and development branch of the galaxy's military-retail empire had been confident that it was on the right track, but had not yet been able to confirm the success of the experiment.

Terran was aware of this unfinished aspect of the time portal's development, but he had had no choice. When the window of opportunity to steal the prototype opened, the Maraudians did not hesitate. Now it would be up to the space pirates to conduct the final experiments needed to fine-tune the phenomenal device to perfection.

"The robots must have been waiting for some lab rats to perform their final experiments," the captain said. "Well, that's not us. Rosario and his men may be the best answer to that problem."

Zalcon agreed. "Yes, Captain, this is the perfect place for the experiment. One way or another, we will engage your plan to loot the ages."

When they arrived on the bridge, the captain gave orders to proceed to their next appointment. Confident that he would return in time for Rosario's rendezvous, the tireless Terran rushed off to meet another counterpart of the Phantom in the China Sea.

Rosario and his crew were more reactive than analytic. They had no idea of the lithe space galleon, the *Maraudor*, that was orbiting high above the Earth, nor could they have understood the solar winds that brought her here. Their pondering never exceeded their present situation. When the space pirates flew away in their sky barge, the buccaneers had no thought beyond the certainty that they would return.

At sunrise, as their ally had promised, their all-night run was rewarded with the silhouette of a treasure ship on the horizon. The predator fleet stayed in formation as it began its pursuit. The light merchantman, which was by no means fast, was under full sail, making for San Juan, still some two hundred miles away. On her present course, she would intersect with the Phantom's fleet within two hours. Although her captain could see the Phantom approaching, he took no evasive action, continuing on his course undaunted.

The steadfast behavior of the gold ship soon became clear to Rosario when three brigs and a brigantine appeared, striking across the horizon in hot pursuit. Running on a broad beam reach, they were maximizing their speed with the appropriate tack. At their present pace, the swift warships would overtake their prize before Rosario could arrive. The Phantom surmised that the desperate captain did not realize that the *Tortuga Diablo* and her escorts were also coming for her gold.

The wily Rosario hoisted the Spanish colors, with the *Blue Dolphin* and *Jewel* quickly following suit. Another of the Phantom's tactics of deception was to cover over the names of his three ships.

As things stood, Rosario would soon have the gold runner bracketed with no hope of escape. At least, that was the plan. But the Phantom knew that a lot could happen between now and then. His flag trick might give him the element of surprise, but the four brigs would still have to be dealt with before he took the prize. Usually, four brigs running together could control any combat situation that might arise. But so long as Rosario had his allies in the sky, he felt confident that he had the advantage.

As the first hour passed, there was still no sign of the space pirates. But the Phantom's fleet was committed, for it was beyond the point of no return. All Rosario could hope for was that the Maraudians would again appear at the last moment to save the day.

It was now mid-morning under a warm golden sun. Brisk trades whipped up a fine mist among sprightly whitecaps as the winds of battle gathered all concerned.

In just a little while, the Phantom would be within range. The first of the brigs was overtaking the gold runner and proceeding to pummel her sails and rigging with a barrage of chain shot. Rosario could only watch this battle. As the chain shot flew through the air, the merchantman came around with the wind.

Under the impression, because of the Spanish colors, that Rosario would be her salvation, the prize unleashed her well-manned battery of cannons. By maneuvering in this way, the wily captain spared his ship the main thrust of the chain shot and suffered negligible damage while inflicting considerable havoc with his return volley of chain shot and eighteen-pounders.

Two of the deadly hull crushers pierced the first brig, the *Batavia*. Under torn and fallen rigging and taking on water, the wounded predator managed to get off a second barrage, which caught the gold runner this time, tearing the aft sails and rigging from her spars. The wounded prey kept running with the wind to meet the second brig. Now Rosario could see her name. She was the *Constant Warrior*, another ship of ill repute from Barataria. Rosario knew the infamous privateer's reputation as a ruthless plunderer and one of many such ships that answered to Lafitte.

Once again, the prize brought the fight to her foe, letting fly with a second barrage as the *Constant Warrior* came to bear. Suddenly, the second brig exploded into toothpicks from a lucky shot into its powder magazine. The tremendous explosion tore the brig from stem to stern, leaving no survivors. Before anyone knew what had happened, the *Constant Warrior* was reduced to smoke and rubble, floating where the great ship had been. Debris fell like rain, missing the Phantom's fleet, but showering the gold runner.

When he saw the *Constant Warrior* disintegrate, Rosario was astonished, as was every other sailor on both sides of the fray. The shock of such instant and complete annihilation froze everyone momentarily.

Refocusing on the *Batavia*, the Phantom realized she was now in range. Her crew was still trying to recover from the first engagement, frantically cutting away the torn rigging, as the *Tortuga Diablo* came to bear. Realizing his inescapable predicament, the enraged captain of the *Batavia* issued a series of impossible commands to his overburdened crew.

Coming by on the same broad reach tack as the merchant-man had, the *Tortuga Diablo* never slowed. She unleashed a full barrage of hull-busters and devastating chain shot to finish off the *Batavia*'s canvas. Precision was the Phantom's trademark.

The *Batavia* would not be leaving the area now or ever. Rosario's barrage left several new holes below the freeboard and reduced the remaining sails to tangled shreds.

But Rosario never came around to finish the *Batavia*; he would leave that to Captain Pizzo. No sooner had the *Tortuga Diablo* delivered her lethal blow than the *Blue Dolphin* bore down on the doomed brig's starboard side. Hoping to get a second volley in before the *Blue Dolphin* was too close, the desperate captain of the *Batavia* unleashed a long-ball barrage against Captain Pizzo. Anticipating the *Batavia*'s intention, Pizzo, who was an elegant sailor, gracefully veered away from the incoming flock of death and destruction before responding in kind. The *Blue Dolphin*'s barrage sealed the *Batavia*'s fate.

By the time the *Dolphin* came alongside the *Batavia*, she was going down. There was chaos on her decks as the crew abandoned ship, jumping into the sea amidst protests and pistol fire from their maddened captain.

The *Blue Dolphin* never slowed. Like Rosario, Pizzo kept running toward the prize.

It was no surprise to see the remaining two brigs break and run. Suddenly, their plan had backfired, and they were outnumbered two to one—or so they thought.

Rosario was greatly relieved with this development, fearing that the brash gold runner was going to get itself sunk. Its actions spoke of a captain who would rather go down with his treasure than give it up.

The fact that Rosario's new partners in the sky had failed to appear was unconscionable. The Phantom knew that his success was due mostly to good luck. Now, as he continued to lure in the prize, these aggravations raged behind his priorities, but he would address them in his own good time.

The unsuspecting merchantman broke off pursuit of the fleeing brigs as they shrank back into the horizon. Rosario continued to close as the gold runner came around on a wide turn that would bring her alongside her rescuer and before the wind. As the two ships approached each other, the *Tortuga Diablo* reefed her sails to make ready for a rendezvous.

Rosario could now see the name of the gold runner. She was the *Cartagena*. Before she came within earshot, Rosario told his crew to act friendly, like one big happy family. Captains Bruno and Pizzo also understood how to play their part. The myriad situations and incidents they had shared over the years had molded the Phantom's crew into a closely knit band of brigands.

The late afternoon turned sultry, with the brisk winds of the day dissipating into a soft breeze, replacing the jostling whitecaps with rolling swells.

Rosario was familiar with this patch of sea, but checked his chart just to be sure.

"Yes," he said, "this will do fine. Helm, come about. Prepare to drop anchor."

"Aye, Captain," responded the helmsman, bringing the *Tortuga Diablo* alongside the *Cartagena* with delicate finesse and dropping anchor.

It was important that the *Tortuga Diablo* drop anchor first, for the gesture suggested that all was well. Rosario then signaled an invitation to dine with the captain. The *Cartagena* took the bait as she, too, dropped anchor and accepted the invitation.

With the afternoon drawing to a close, all four ships lay in close anchorage. Captains Pizzo and Bruno were already aboard the *Tortuga Diablo* when the dinghy from the *Cartagena* arrived. Rosario had ample time to brief his officers on what he had in mind for his dinner guests.

"We'll keep the surprise until the last possible moment," he said. "I want to take them with as little fuss as possible."

While the launch from the *Cartagena* was tying up to the *Tortuga*, Rosario summed up his plan to Rodriguez. "That's what buccaneering is all about," he said, "capturing treasure, not sinking it!"

The party of three that came aboard included the first mate, the second mate, and the boatswain. To the Phantom's surprise, their captain was not among them.

After introductions, the first mate explained, "I'm afraid our good captain was gravely wounded in the second barrage, and he was dead before the brig exploded."

"I'm sorry for your loss," Rosario said. "I'm sure he'd be glad to know your cargo is still intact."

"Aye," said the first mate. "He was resigned to go down with the ship before surrendering. It was the grace of God that brought you to us just in time." It seemed that he could not say enough to express his gratitude and relief.

While the Phantom's battle tactics had been intimidating, it was the *Cartagena* that had issued the fatal blow, a fact that went unnoticed by the three grateful sailors as they praised the men of the *Tortuga*.

"Please thank your men for their gallantry, Captain," said the second mate, as his boatswain nodded eagerly.

Rosario let them emote as he continued the guise of the dinner party well past sunset. He and his officers found the first mate to be an admirable salt, ruddy and robust, and in command of a winning sense of humor. Nimbly fielding the often quizzical remarks of the Phantom's high command, he stayed loyal all the while to his dead captain by skillfully keeping the subject of his cargo out of the conversation. Quick-witted and amusing, he spoke of his past years as a boatswain. His name was Robert Plant, a Brit.

Knowing his golden secret, Rosario and his two captains pretended to stumble innocently upon the avoided subject. Each time one of them brought up the subject of treasure, the coy Mr. Plant creatively diverted attention to some humorous, seemingly related story.

The Phantom and his officers thoroughly enjoyed themselves with these likable sailors, but business was business, and it was time to take care of it. Rosario let the warm, light-hearted sounds of the dinner party reverberate into silence before completely extinguishing the mood. Now that the moment was at hand, he came hard about.

"It was indeed your good fortune," he said, "that we came along when we did."

The men of the *Cartagena* looked at Rosario quizzically. It seemed a little odd to reopen the subject of their rescue after they had already covered that topic so lavishly. Nonetheless, Mr. Plant took it in stride.

"Yes, Captain," he said, "we wouldn't be enjoying this fine dinner, if not for your most timely appearance."

Rosario answered, "Yes, at least this way you and your crew get away with your ship and your lives."

The three dinner guests sat stunned in icy realization of their situation. Rosario's words had ripped the warm atmosphere from the room, freezing the moment and the mood. Suddenly things were making new sense. Rosario's timely appearance had not been a coincidence.

Plant looked up at the already smiling Rosario. "Who *are* you?" he asked.

"I'm sure you've heard of the Phantom, gentlemen," Pizzo said. When they nodded, he added, "You are now in his hands."

The Phantom's tanned face took on a compelling expression in the amber light of the grand cabin. The rich golden flush of confidence on his darkened features told the men from the *Cartagena* the prize was lost. Realizing he had been duped, the first mate sank back in resignation. Rosario and his captains exchanged smug glances. It was obvious that the spirited Mr. Plant would not be causing any trouble.

"What now?" asked the second mate, thoroughly disheartened.

"Although we are prepared to do whatever must be done," the Phantom replied matter-of-factly, "my men and I would be very happy to just take the gold and let you go on your way. I'm sure you'll agree any further resistance would fail. Can I count on you to cooperate in exchange for your ship and your freedom?"

All three sailors nodded. Now that they knew they were in the clutches of the Phantom, they were not surprised by his benevolence regarding their lives and their vessel. Plant made a subdued but earnest utterance of their gratitude.

"We appreciate the uncommon kindness, sir," he said, "for which you are rightly famous."

As a full ochre moon rose out of the sea into a clear starlit night, Rosario had still not been contacted by Terran. He hoped the absence meant that the Maraudians were not coming back. He wished it could be that simple.

Terran had more than one iron in the fire. Offloading his latest prize had taken longer than usual. He got under way after the haul was safely stored aboard the mother ship. When he returned from the Sea of Siam, his first reports were of the battle that was taking place at the rendezvous point. That he was late again for his appointment to plunder was of little concern to the preoccupied space pirate. His dealings on the other side of this wealthy little planet justified remaining longer than anticipated. Appropriation of treasure was the priority. If the Phantom's present mission should fail, Terran would find another opportunity and other means. Either way, the prize would not escape him.

When he arrived at the rendezvous site, seeing that the Phantom's fleet surrounded the *Cartagena* in close anchorage, Terran was confident that Rosario was in command of the situation below. Remaining undetected, he tracked the two brigs that had broken off from the engagement.

Using every stitch of canvas and running with the wind, the two brigs hoped to intercept the second gold runner undisturbed. Feeling the thrill of their hunt as they sailed through the night toward their prize, the crews of the Corsair's ships had no idea they were being watched like prey by vultures from space.

"They have very accurate intelligence," Zalcon remarked. "Their intersecting course could not be more direct. It would not be the first time that treasure came wrapped in treachery."

Zalcon was right. Running with a broad reach, the ravenous privateers would soon raise the second gold runner.

Just after sunrise, the large merchantman appeared on the horizon. When he sighted the two brigs of the Corsair's fleet, Captain Fiott of the *Hartwell* executed a 180-degree turn in a desperate attempt to flee. However, running before the wind would not maximize her speed. The massive ship was slow compared to the swift brigs bearing down on her.

By mid-morning, both predators were overtaking the gold runner. She was one of the largest ships of her kind, and loaded with gold bullion, silver, and Incan artifacts encrusted with jewels, all on their way to Liverpool. But it was not the ancient Incan artifacts that alerted the space pirates. Their stolen scanners only reacted to gold and several kinds of precious stone.

These artifacts would have a certain value in their distant galaxy of countless planets peopled with ravenous consumers. However, they would be secondary to the twelve hundred bars of gold bullion contained within the *Hartwell*'s hold.

In the entire expanse of space that Terran was aware of, gold was the most valuable object, above all others except one. Gold was far more available than the ultimate possession. Only the legendary Esseen Crystals were superior to pure gold. In fact, the crystals were so rare that many had ceased to believe in their existence.

Legend said that the Lamorians were the keepers of the sacred crystals, whose properties afforded a miraculous existence and eternal youth. Every Maraudian knew the legend of Lamoria and the cradle race, those first humans who migrated so long ago from their garden planet. Their offspring had peopled the Qwarzarian galaxy—and probably this one, too.

Although no one ever expected to come into contact with the fabulous crystals, Terran knew what to look for. If he ever saw one, he would recognize a Lamorian timeship, which was the chalice for the divine elements. It was no coincidence that Maraudian sky barges resembled Lamorian design. As unlikely as it seemed, the thought of one day finding the Esseen Crystals was the secret hope of all Maraudians.

The ancient planet Qwarz was believed to be the cradle planet of the countless peopled planets in the parsec of space that Terran called home. It was there that the phenomenal jade hieroglyphs of the Lamorians were located. The many messages they possessed had remained in the sacred Valley of Siniah, indelible for a time that could only be called endless. There, every day that the Qwarzarian sun shone, the miraculous jade tablets projected vivid, highly detailed holographs, proof and promise of the existence of the Lamorians and the Esseen crystals.

An extensive stay in the Valley of Siniah was one of the requirements to complete what the Maraudians considered the highest level of education.

Terran and his officers knew the ancient messages thoroughly. They would easily recognize anything that spoke of Lamoria and her magic. There was no hint of the rare jewels of Lamoria being here on this tiny treasure planet or in its newly discovered galaxy. But there was an ample amount of the next best thing— gold!

The *Hartwell* was like a sitting duck as the Corsair's two surviving frigates closed in for the kill. Again, their success seemed to be a foregone conclusion, just as it had been on the previous day when they were foiled in the eleventh hour of their pursuit. This time, however, there were no ships or visible means of interference as Lafitte's privateers commenced their attack.

With his ship wrapped in a thick overcast, Terran was able to observe the fracas as it unfolded.

Realizing that escape was not an option, Captain Fiott brought the *Hartwell* around and unleashed her twenty-one starboard cannons on the *Orient* as it continued to close upon him. The *Hartwell* had been too hasty to catch the up roll, so its salvo fell just short of the undaunted assailant. A second barrage was let loose from the *Hartwell's* portside battery at the *Hussar* as the second brig came into close range. Catching at least a dozen of the twenty-one cannonballs hurled at her, the *Hussar* suffered moderate damage and slowed.

Before the *Hartwell* could fire another barrage, the *Orient,* unscathed and well in range, let fly a horrendous firestorm of chain shot into the sails and rigging of the doomed treasure ship. The insidious fragmentation ripped through the rigging and crew alike, leaving the weather deck of the *Hartwell* strewn with casualties and debris, ruining her ability to retaliate.

Terran watched with delight as the two predators disabled the prize. With a delicate finesse, they paralyzed the great ship while preserving the hull's integrity and her precious cargo. Disabled and taking on water, the lumbering *Hussar* came alongside and strafed the *Hartwell's* decks with a second maelstrom of grapeshot.

Another barrage from the *Orient* tore most of the remaining sails from their spars, leaving the *Hartwell* dead in the water. By midday, the sea battle was all but over as the desperate and battered crew of the *Hartwell* prepared to repel boarders.

Simultaneously, dozens of grappling hooks came in on the *Hartwell* from port and starboard, too many for the besieged frigate to repel. After tossing several grenades, all hands on both brigs, armed to the teeth, stood ready and eager to board the prize and feed the flames of this day, which would see them all in hell.

The Maraudians appeared unnoticed over the fray as the warm midday sun evaporated the dense fog.

Captain Terran, reassessing the situation below, chose his first target. While Lafitte's privateers swarmed aboard the treasure ship, Terran fired his two sonic cannons at the *Orient*. The powerful pulsation pounded the brig, snapping her great masts in half like matchsticks. Sails and rigging toppled down on the decks already covered with bewildered sailors.

The next to succumb to the devastating weapon was the *Hartwell*. Again, the hideous sound preceded the impact of the destructive burst. The broken spars fell, covering the mass of combatants, most of whom lay dazed all over the weather deck of the derelict gold ship. A third blast, while not unlike the others, ended the crew's hopes for survival, sealing the *Hussar*'s fate, as everyone aboard lay dead.

As Terran watched all this, the science officer's voice came over the ship's speakers.

"Mandoon to Captain Terran! …Sir, we've had a breakthrough! Please come to the science deck as soon as possible!"

Before hurrying back to the orbiting mother ship, Zalcon said to Terran, "The living down there may be able to recover and cause problems for Rosario when he arrives."

After considering this for a moment, Terran left no survivors.

A full day had passed since the Phantom's fleet had fought the sea battle that was unattended by his new ally.

The crew members of the *Cartagena* were confined below deck until their entire shipment of gold bullion was offloaded.

While their men secured the bullion, Rosario and his captains conferred on the flagship.

"The other brigs," said Captain Bruno, "probably knew about the second gold ship."

"And no doubt are looting it as we speak," said Pizzo.

"Be that as it may," said Rosario, "I count my blessings for the way things have turned out. We got lucky when that second brig blew up. If we never see our partners from the sky again, so much the better. On the other hand, if they do show up, it will be interesting to see how they justify an even split in this latest haul when half is no doubt already lost to Lafitte."

By sunrise, Rosario's fleet was running before the wind, keeping a keen lookout for any signs of the second treasure ship. All morning, the three ships sailed as one under densely overcast skies. The favorable winds would soon put them in the vicinity of the second prize. Rosario was sure he would see Terran by then.

Back on the *Maraudor*, Mandoon had Terran's and Zalcon's undivided attention as he demonstrated his latest revelations on the time device.

"From what I now understand," he said, "we will be able to take a single sailing ship and its crew back or forward in time by simply placing the portal in the middle of it."

"You mean, we can use *their* ships as well?" asked Zalcon, obviously excited by Mandoon's discoveries. "That means we could send them back without telling them."

"Yes, indeed," Terran agreed, "it *would* be easier if we didn't have to explain too much."

"We will have to actually *use* the device to understand it further," Mandoon explained. "The time spike might not be evident to the Illuminosity if we only travel a short distance...say, one hundred years or so."

"So long as you believe we will not be detected," said Terran, "I will try it."

Terran always rationalized his decision to take a risk when a prize was worth it.

"Of course," Mandoon continued, "there is still the problem of cerebral abrasions. I think they're caused by some variable I have not yet discovered. Only field testing will solve this mystery as well, Captain."

"We will need to find some records," said Zalcon. "Some indications of when and where the treasure troves of a hundred years ago may be."

It was not his good looks that made Zalcon the first mate of the *Maraudor*. It was his quick wit that whisked him along as the three men worked out where they would find such records.

Terran did not want to ask Rosario directly. "I wouldn't want him to get any ideas," he said.

As the afternoon wore on, the three space pirates concocted a plan and a story that would achieve their goals. They would locate the largest ship they could commandeer, mount sonic cannons on her, and send her along with her unsuspecting crew of buccaneers back into the past. They began at once to prepare for this experiment. First, they would need an appropriate ship. Then they would have to teach the surface sailors how to use the sonic cannon.

It was time to rendezvous with Rosario and plan his next mission. As the sky barge separated from the mother ship and started down, Terran and Zalcon continued to work out the details. The grey ceiling was much lower than usual, concealing the Maraudians as they hovered high above the fleet, from where Terran could see that Rosario was heading for the last known location of the quarry.

Soon after the Phantom arrived at the anticipated point of interception, the second treasure ship and one of the brigs appeared on the horizon. The *Hussar* was nowhere in sight. The two ships seemed to be in close quarters. Soon, the lookout could see the wrecked decks of both the *Hartwell* and the *Orient*, but could not detect any movement on either ship.

By the time the fleet arrived at the site, it was clear that what had occurred was the mark of Terran. The Maraudians had left quite a piece of finished work. It was a doleful scene, speaking of the space pirates' indifference to human life.

The galleon and the brig were listing, entangled in torn rigging and grappling hooks. Both crews lay motionless on the weather decks as the rolling swells rocked them like a cradle in their endless sleep.

Now Rosario could see the remnants of the *Hussar*, which were all but submerged. Only the aft weather deck remained above the waterline.

The Phantom dispatched Captain Pizzo to the *Orient*, while he and Captain Bruno prepared to board the *Hartwell*. Rosario kept looking up, expecting to see Terran at any moment. Even though this mission was a success, he could not help feeling disappointed about the way things had worked out. He would have gladly sacrificed this second prize if it meant the end of his precarious partnership with the Maraudians.

The Phantom's crew worked for the rest of the day, unloading the bullion and any relics that contained jewels or gold. Captain Pizzo discovered a sizable cache of gold and gems aboard the *Orient*, in a remote storage hold below the second deck. Unlike the galleon, where there was treasure stored everywhere, the stash found on the brig was a little known fact, hidden under empty rum casks and burlap sacks. It was the captain's personal stash. Pizzo waited until he joined Rosario and Bruno below decks on the broken *Hartwell* to report the *Orient*'s surprise.

"Three chests," he said, "full of diamonds, rubies, sapphires, and pearls, and eight chests of gold doubloons. We should keep this little surprise a secret. After all, *we're* doing all the fighting and dying down here!"

Rosario considered Pizzo's idea, but decided against holding out on his partners. "They probably know about the *Orient*'s stash," he said, "the same way they seem to know everything else."

Captain Bruno agreed. "We don't know enough about what these buzzards can do," he said, "and until we do, we should play it straight."

"Agreed," said Rosario. "What Terran did here justifies his claim to half the prize…, and it would behoove us to say nothing to the contrary."

An hour before sunset, the overcast cleared, revealing the *Maraudor*'s sky barge hovering over the Phantom's fleet. The familiar hemp basket lowered as before, carrying Terran and his first mate.

Again, Rosario gave last-minute instructions to his officers and crew as they watched the Maraudians descend.

"Remember," he cried, "one big happy family!"

Rosario's mind had never changed. Although he had been lucky in the last mission, he knew that as far as these sky pirates were concerned, he and his crew were expendable.

The image of the hovering sky barge against the fading blue sky of flaming crimson bands was as stunning as it was intimidating as the Phantom pondered the treacherous position he was in.

When the space captain and his first mate stepped aboard,

Rosario greeted them with gusto: "Captain Terran, Commander Zalcon, welcome!"

The formalities had barely been observed when the space pirates got down to business. With only a brief eye contact greeting, the Maraudians became preoccupied with their share of the spoils, which they had Rosario's crew offload immediately.

Moving on to the secondary cache, Terran asked, "Anything of interest on the *Orient*?"

Throwing a glance at Pizzo, Rosario responded without hesitation, "As a matter of fact, there was." And he proceeded to recite the precise inventory of the find.

As Terran listened, his impassive expression did not reveal that Rosario's candid response confirmed his opinion that the Phantom could be trusted to be a man of his word.

Terran's matter-of-fact reception also confirmed Rosario's suspicions that the space pirates could see treasure from above.

Another fantastic tool of theirs, no doubt. If that is indeed the case, they may know where MY *treasure trove is hidden.*

These thoughts twisted another knot in Rosario's stomach as he played his part and bided his time.

After inspecting and dividing all the fresh booty, the captains and officers took up the matter of their next conquest.

"It will be a training exercise as well as a paying venture," said Terran. "I suggest we install a sonic cannon aboard one of your ships, Captain."

Rosario could not believe his ears.

They're offering me one of their fantastic cannons! It seems suspicious, but it's an opportunity I can't refuse.

Curbing his emotion, Rosario said, "The *Jewel* is best suited. She'll hold more than the other two combined." It was only because the *Tortuga Diablo* had a deep sentimental value to Rosario that he did not use the *Jewel* as his flagship. "I assume you will teach my crew to man the gun."

"You will easily be able to vanquish any opposition," Terran said, "once your crew masters the controls. It will take Lieutenant Zane little more than a week to train them in all they will need to know."

Delighted with this plan, Rosario gave it his consent and said no more as he brought out some rum and offered it to his guests.

To his surprise, they flatly refused.

"Water is the only thing suitable for drinking," said Terran.

Rosario could see in his eyes that he considered the consumption of rum, or spirits in general, an act of inferior judgment.

Strange pirates, indeed!

But he kept his thoughts to himself, showing no offense.

By the time this meeting concluded, it was well past sunset on a moonless night. The ship's lanterns barely illuminated the hemp gondola, which was waiting on the *Tortuga Diablo*'s forward weather deck. As Terran and Zalcon climbed into the basket, Rosario looked up into the black night.

Just then, a shaft of golden light, too bright for its source to be seen, shot down from directly over the landing party, startling all hands.

The awesome sight held Rosario mystified.

This must be another of their wondrous tools!

As the hemp basket ascended, Rosario and the others watched it rise into the light until Terran and Zalcon reached the sky barge. And then suddenly there was only total darkness once again.

The Phantom and his crew found it hard to sleep that night as fears, suspicions, and superstitions ravaged the imaginations of these simple Earthbound sailors.

Are they devils?

Have we been cursed?

Is Terran Lucifer himself?

What will become of us?

We'll be lucky to escape with our lives!

Terror was no stranger to any of the Phantom's handpicked crew. But after all they had been through, this alliance with Terran was showing them a new level of fear that threatened to dissolve their courage.

The next few days were uneventful as the men constructed the large struts necessary to accommodate the strange new weapon from Marauda. After installing the huge sonic cannon on the bow of the *Jewel*, Rosario's gun crew trained for twelve days under Lieutenant Zane's direction to master the space weapon.

Every morning, once Zane was aboard, the sky barge would take off, not to be seen again until day's end.

Where do they go every day? Rosario wondered. *What are*

they up to? And why does Zane keep having my men practice the same stupid drill over and over?

For hours at a time, Zane made the crew turn the gun and aim it, but never fire.

"Aiming is the tricky part," he would say. "Remember, always aim at the center of what you want to hit to get your best spread. For ships, if you aim at the freeboard, you will sink the target before you will ever have a chance to board her. And there is no way to find her, once she goes under, is there? To render the quarry dead in the water but still afloat, aim at the center point of the masts. As you develop a feel for aiming, you will be able to burst or preserve any part of any hull. But for now, play it safe and aim high."

Rosario chose Will Knox, the boatswain, to be commander of the space cannon crew. Finding Lieutenant Zane's instructions easy to understand, Knox demonstrated a flawless technique. The boatswain found it odd that the basic workings of the wonder weapon, loading and cleaning, were never addressed by Zane, nor did he make any mention of the initial procedures to prepare the cannon for action. It seemed to be always at the ready.

There were three intensity settings to choose from before firing. The first notch delivered a blast that would daze a life form temporarily, but had no effect on inanimate material. The second notch delivered a blast that caused cellular disintegration within a three-foot radius and a severe concussive effect within a hundred-foot radius. This was the intensity that had been used on the previous missions and was recommended for all situations except when total obliteration was necessary, for which only the third intensity would suffice.

Rosario listened carefully as Zane explained the dos and don'ts of the weapon.

"I repeat," Zane said, "once the prize goes under, it's lost."

Knox and his men nodded in acknowledgment as Rosario was suddenly swept up in revelation.

That's it! That's what I was looking for. He's just admitted that they can't find treasure when it's under water…. If that's true, there might yet be a chance to come out on top with these rogues.

"We'll be watching over you, lads, no worries," Zane concluded. "After your first mission, you'll be experts! Just aim and fire the way I showed you, and you'll be as smart as any in no time."

Zane's words sat well with the novice gun crew as their time to go into action drew near.

That night, Knox conferred with his captain.

"I still don't know 'ow to ready the weapon for action," he said. "We can aim and fire it alright. But without one of 'em to make it ready, we could never bring it to bear."

Rosario was not surprised. "They're no dunderheads," he replied. "They don't want us turning the tables on *them*. Keep a close eye, learn its secrets. There's treachery afoot, to be sure."

Knox looked deep into Rosario's eyes and nodded.

Indeed, at this very moment, the double-dealing Terran

was concluding his third rendezvous with none other than Jean Lafitte. Presenting himself to the Corsair in much the same way as he had done to Rosario, Terran had the King of Barataria in line to loot Rosario's secret treasure trove while the Phantom was busy preparing the *Jewel*.

Lafitte jumped at the chance to strike at Rosario's heart. Terran told him to use at least four large ships to carry everything. The Corsair agreed to all of Terran's ideas and was beside himself with this opportunity. With Terran's charts, Lafitte would deal a devastating blow to the Phantom by making off with the fruits of eleven years of buccaneering.

"No worries," Terran assured Lafitte. "Should Rosario interfere, I will neutralize him and his ships."

Drunk with the idea, the Corsair agreed to the mission and was under way in forty-eight hours, taking four large galleons toward that remote island that was the bank of Rosario.

As pirates go, the Phantom was unique when it came to wealth. Rosario still had half of the treasure from his first haul. Eleven years of this type of collecting had amassed a treasure trove, the likes of which the awestruck Corsair could not have imagined. In the time it took to train the new gun crew of the *Jewel*, Lafitte and his fleet went unhindered as they found and looted every bit of the Phantom's fabulous plunder.

It was Commander Zalcon's idea to use the Corsair to get the treasure out of the volcano hideaway into the open, and then let Rosario attack the dupes with the *Jewel* and her new gun. Terran admired Zalcon's ability to always come up with strategies that not only expedited the operations, but also yielded a generous profit. This caper would retrieve half of Rosario's fabulous cache immediately upon collecting their share from Lafitte. Later on, should the Phantom realize he was stealing his own booty, the Maraudians could blame the theft on the Corsair and still be within their rights to an equal share. Using one pirate against another was the art of their treachery and a constant source of delight. When this heist was over, Rosario would have assisted Terran in securing seventy-five percent of his own fabulous treasure trove.

The Corsair was elated with the ease and success of this extraordinary mission. Terran's estimate of four treasure galleons was precisely what was needed to contain all the booty they recovered.

As he was returning to Barataria, Lafitte was visited by his new partners from the sky. After two full days of offloading, Terran had his half secured. This concluded his plans for the Corsair. Before leaving, he told Lafitte of another treasure ship that was nearby and unprotected. Terran persuaded the Corsair to intercept it with his two empty galleons. Then, with the Maraudians' assistance, Lafitte could collect the additional treasure before returning to Barataria. The Corsair was eager to undertake another profitable venture.

After waving farewell to Lafitte, Terran and Zalcon exchanged snide glances, for they were sending the Corsair on a wild goose chase. At this moment, the infamous Lafitte might have claimed that his heist of Rosario's treasure was the crowning jewel of all his adventures. In reality, the king of Barataria had seen much better days.

As Lafitte sailed off, he was confident that his next engagement would be another bonanza, never suspecting that treachery was in the wind. The pirates of Marauda were about to bring his escapades to an abrupt end in a fatal hurricane.

The Maraudians were excited by the mass of treasure this tiny world was yielding. Their discovery had been a rare stroke of luck. Deposits of gold and treasure in the quantities they were accumulating far surpassed those of any of the other planets in Terran's prior experience. In the Maraudians' past, there had been more than a few missions that had a much smaller yield at a much greater cost. The mere presence of such opulence gave them an uncontrollable sense of avarice as they worked harder and harder to loot all they could manage.

This altered state of urgency that overtook them was genetic, a natural mechanism in the minds of all Maraudians. Seldom pondered, this instinctual frenzy was known as the Rapture. Deep in its throes, Terran and his officers put together their wildest plan yet.

On the last day of training, before he left with Zane, Zalcon conferred with Rosario and his captains in the grand cabin of the *Jewel*.

"At these coordinates," he said, pointing to a map on the

table, "we have discovered two treasure galleons making for the Straits of Florida. They will provide an excellent opportunity for you to try out your new weapon."

"My men will make short work of it," said Captain Bruno. "We can be there in a few hours."

"Our business here is done," said Zalcon. "I only have some final adjustments to make to the cannon."

When the five officers arrived at the bow, Zalcon stood over the weapon's controls so as to block what he was doing.

After a moment, he turned to Rosario and said, "The cannon is now ready for action…and will remain so for two days before shutting down again."

The Phantom's fleet got under way as the sky barge disappeared into the sky. By midmorning, it lay in wait on the leeside of Andros Island. Rosario planned to come in behind the two gold runners as they entered the straits. Zalcon never mentioned where these two treasure ships were coming from, only that they were heading south.

Standing on the quarterdeck with Rodriguez, Rosario was tormented, his mind ablaze with questions, his every instinct protesting the mission. It soon became clear that both men were sharing the same thoughts.

Rodriguez was first to point out the most obvious fact about the mission. "There's no doubt," he said, "these gold runners belong to Lafitte. Makes one wonder where they might be coming from…, if you know what I mean."

Grimacing, Rosario nodded and grumbled his agreement.

They didn't have long to wait before the prize appeared off the starboard bow. A fresh wind whisked the Phantom's fleet into position. One galleon took the point ahead of the other as they came around to face their assailants.

"Captain," said Rodriguez, "it looks like they mean to fight it out with us!"

Obviously, the galleons' desperate commanders had elected to fight their way out of this unwelcome situation. A bold maneuver perhaps, but Rosario knew they had also made a smart move. The lumbering galleons had every stitch of sail pulling them faster than ever before, but they were still no match for the Phantom. Lafitte's ships had substantial firepower, with forty cannons each, and would waste no time in using them.

A steady breeze hustled the *Jewel* over the rolling swells toward the engagement. The *Tortuga Diablo* and the *Blue Dolphin* followed at a close distance, ready to reinforce as needed. All eyes waited with keen anticipation as the gun crew prepared to unleash the incisive weapon on their first real target.

After a long inspection, Rodriguez lowered the telescope from his eye. "I can see no identiying marks and there are no colors flying, Captain."

"No matter," said Rosario. "They could only belong to Lafitte. I'm certain of that."

"*Si*, Captain," said Rodriguez, "and once again, our partners in the sky are nowhere to be seen."

"Why does this not surprise me?" asked Rosario.

In fact, Terran was preparing Rosario's fleet for their next mission. He would leave them on their own to bag the quarry and demonstrate their newly acquired expertise.

Will Knox thoroughly understood the operational procedures of the weapon. Nevertheless, this would be his first time applying his new skill in a combat situation.

On the *Maraudor*, Zalcon was concluding his update to Terran with a suggestion. "Captain," he said, "I think we should send Mandoon on this first time mission. He is essential to its success. He alone knows how to operate the time portal and it would give him the best opportunity to solve the remaining mysteries of the device."

Zalcon's recommendation needed little consideration by Terran. He had already come to the same conclusion.

While Knox's gun crew had been training on the *Jewel*, and the Corsair had been off looting the bank of Rosario, Terran had visited the Hall of Records in Jamaica to acquire a book known as the Gazetteer. He was listening to his first officer's summation as he pondered the great book's comprehensive list. The Gazetteer included departure dates and destinations of wrecked treasure ships from the past one hundred and fifty years.

Among the list of eighteenth-century candidates, one in particular stood out: the *Preciado*, a Spanish galleon out of Maricaibo, loaded with gold bullion and silver. Accompanying her were two Spanish frigates, the *Prince* and the *Ortega*, formidable protection for the massive fortune as the Spaniards made their way home. The Gazetteer showed that the *Preciado* and her escorts had fallen victim to the fleet of the infamous pirate, Blackbeard. This account went on to say that the *Revenge*, a sloop of the British Navy, intercepted this most relentless of all buccaneers, and slew him in a massive sea battle just days after the *Preciado* was lost.

Realizing that he had found the perfect target, Terran grinned, a sharp contrast to his usual stern expression. But, like a shooting star that no one witnessed, this special moment slipped by unnoticed.

Zalcon followed his captain's finger as it silently pointed out the *Preciado*'s listing in the stolen Gazetteer. As their eyes met again, it was Zalcon who wore the smirk of the picaroon. This would be the *Maraudor*'s first reach into the past, and a shining example of the great riches awaiting such timely visits.

Mandoon had made some progress, claiming that his experiments had revealed the device's ability to travel relatively short periods of time unnoticed by the Illuminosity. But was this invisibility relative to all of time or just a few hours? That was the pressing unanswerable question. As far as Mandoon could tell, a hundred years should be safe. The space wizard also had a working hypothesis for the reentry problem.

Terran's decision to send Mandoon back in time on their first mission was final.

Needless to say, Mandoon was none too thrilled with his orders to accompany Rosario and the other expendables on the perilous venture.

"If anything happens to me," he protested, "you'll be without a science officer!"

Zalcon chuckled to himself. *If that's the only reason he can come up with, he doesn't stand a chance at changing Terran's mind.*

Terran now turned Zalcon's attention to the charts he was studying. Pointing to the narrow straits between the Great Abaco Islands and the tiny Cartan Islands, he explained, "Here is where they will sink the *Preciado* with whatever treasure they cannot fit aboard the *Jewel*. It's only seven fathoms deep at this point. Aside from the two-day sail north, it is the perfect spot. Our prize should go unhindered through the decades and appear here with us as Rosario and Mandoon return from the mission."

"Aye, Captain. Unless we try, we'll never know."

A last glance at the charts concluded the top-level reconnoiter. The plan was as simple as it was fantastic.

On his way back to his quarters, the insightful first officer was already consumed with problems that could arise if the expendables should get any ideas of their own.

Aboard Lafitte's remaining two treasure ships, the piercing cry of the boatswain's whistle sent all hands scrambling to their stations for the inevitable battle.

As Rosario's fleet came within range, his suspicions were

confirmed. These ships were the *Bernice* and the *Concepción*, two ill reputes from Barataria.

On the *Jewel*, the mood was more sporting than fighting as Rosario snapped the crew into focus.

"Stay with it till it's over, mates! No mistakes, lads, stay sharp!"

Confident that the sonic cannons would be more than sufficient, the Phantom did not bother to have his conventional weapons manned and ready.

Will Knox and his anxious novices waited for their captain's order to fire as they closed on the target. Rosario would wait until the *Bernice* came around to issue her barrage before he showed the frantic galleon his surprise.

Aiming the wonder weapon as the *Bernice* came to bear, Knox intended to topple only her aft masts. A double shot at the same point would neutralize the ship and severely stun her crew.

The *Concepción* followed closely behind the *Bernice* in their desperate attempt to fight their way out. The Phantom's fleet continued closing on the *Bernice* as she strained to get her cannons lined up. Finally, she swerved to port and came around. The massive galleon lost precious moments to take her shot as she settled and waited for the up roll. The *Jewel* would fire on the *Bernice* just as she came to bear. The moment was at hand.

"Fire!"

As soon as Rosario issued the command, Knox squeezed the trigger.

Nothing happened.

The boatswain squeezed the trigger again—repeatedly—but the wonder weapon stood silent as the *Bernice* unleashed a thunderstorm of chain shot and hull busters.

Instinctively, Rosario swerved to port in an attempt to outrun the firestorm. The galleon's barrage ripped into the *Jewel*, catching her sailors by surprise and tearing her aft sails to shreds, while several cannonballs perforated her freeboard.

Suddenly, the tables were turned on the Phantom. Relying on Terran's weapon had proven to be a terrible mistake as Rosario's crew frantically manned the ship's cannons, knowing that the *Bernice* would easily get off another barrage before they could be ready to return fire.

Mortified, Knox finally realized the cause of the malfunction. On this, their first field action, his crew had forgotten to select one of the three intensity settings. The lever was still in the off position. Now, well within range, the *Bernice* would soon be ready to fire a fatal barrage. Knox quickly corrected the problem, but failed to readjust his aim as he squeezed the trigger repeatedly. Instantly, he heard the now familiar sound of the sonic haymaker. All of the galleon's masts snapped in half, falling into a snarl of canvas and rigging.

Beneath the strewn debris were the motionless bodies of the crew. In his excitement, Knox had fired no less than four separate sonic barrages, eliminating any chance of human survivors. The derelict galleon slowed to a drift as the *Blue Dolphin* came alongside.

While the *Tortuga Diablo* and the wounded *Jewel* chased the *Concepción*, Rosario dispatched the *Blue Dolphin* to offload the *Bernice* as it drifted in silence. The great treasure galleon had become a floating funeral pyre, replete with a full crew of corpses.

The second treasure galleon, the *Concepción*, had come about, and was running before the wind in a fated attempt to escape the unscathed *Tortuga Diablo*. The midday action stretched into a late balmy afternoon as the inevitable took a few more hours. The *Tortuga Diablo* and the *Jewel* bracketed the overloaded treasure galleon as she lumbered hopelessly under full sail. Faster than the galleon, even when wounded, the *Jewel* caught up to her. The sonic cannon would make short work of the first phase of this mission, but there would still be much to do before this goldfish was caught, cleaned, and stored. As the *Jewel* made her final approach, the *Tortuga Diablo* closed the distance on the *Concepción*—the largest of the fifty ships in the Corsair's fleet.

Terrified by what had happened to the *Bernice* and realizing the hopelessness of his situation, the captain of the *Concepción* decided not to do what Lafitte would have expected of him. Instead, he hoisted the white flag and turned the galleon into the wind.

As the *Tortuga Diablo* and the *Jewel* came alongside, Captain Bruno hailed the crew of the *Concepción*, demanding that they abandon the galleon in their small boats.

This request was met with passionate resistance. The officers and men of the *Concepción* were hanging from the elaborate superstructure and lined up all along the weather deck, waving and pleading with the Phantom: "Take our treasure, but leave us our ship!"

Obviously, they knew of the Phantom's benevolent reputation. But even on his best day, Rosario would not have had much consideration for the men or ships of the Corsair. When Bruno shouted that the command was not open for discussion, their riotous response caused Rosario to order Knox to readjust the sonic cannon to the lowest intensity and fire a triple blast amidships.

When the high-pitched blast rang out, every sailor on the *Concepción* collapsed in silence.

Knox looked up at Rosario, awaiting further orders.

"Are they dead?" the Phantom asked.

"As far as I know, Captain, they should still be alive."

Rosario nodded. Then, turning to Rodriguez, he said, "Let's get on with it!"

The first mate pressed his men into action, but Rosario was uneasy, a feeling he recognized as trouble. He wanted this day to be over.

The *Tortuga Diablo* let fly her grappling hooks and tied up on the *Concepción*'s portside as the *Jewel* came up on her starboard side.

Not long after Rosario's men boarded the *Concepción*, her stunned crew started to stir. However, it was obvious that it would still be a while before they were back on their feet.

Because the *Jewel* had sustained considerable damage, Rosario decided to commandeer the *Concepción* rather than offload its fabulous treasure. The befuddled crew would be set adrift in lifeboats.

"What are we going to do with this galleon now that we have it?" Rodriguez asked.

Rosario was quick to answer. "We have no need of such a large and slow member in our nimble fleet, but I'm sure we'll think of something."

Suddenly, they heard a woman screaming from deep within the galleon. The men turned as one and scrambled below to find her. As they reached the remote storage hold, the salts were met with a vision of loveliness that far surpassed anything they had ever seen before. Moreover, the stunning beauty was not in any way suffering from the effects of the sonic blasts.

The Phantom's reaction was no different than any of the other men when he felt that scream slice through him. Normally, Rosario would wait for a report on a disturbance, but the passion in the woman's shrill outcry drew him below to investigate for himself. When he arrived, he found the men sheepishly quiet, reverently gazing into the deep dark pools that were the goddess's eyes.

Upon discovering this enchanting creature, Rosario was instantly swept away, as if by a tidal wave, his mind swimming with a delicious passion.

Knox broke the awkward silence. "She seems sound enough, Cap'n. The weapon ain't bothered *'er* none."

Somehow, Knox was unaffected by the beauty's presence. His words were a lifeline, pulling his captain back into the moment. Rosario was still breathless when the goddess spoke.

"Are you indeed the captain of these men?"

Their eyes met as her question rolled off her lips, filling him with desire.

"I am," he said. "Captain Rosario, at your service."

The irresistible being responded, "I am Aleia. I was the captain's woman. If you are the captain of these men, then I belong to you now."

Trying to listen to her words, Rosario found it hard to focus as hundreds of notions that had long been dormant within him were now demanding an immediate audience. Surely, the age-old taboo of bringing a woman to sea did not apply to her. She spoke with a courtly eloquence in velvet tones that captivated the Phantom, once again leaving him momentarily speechless.

Offering her his hand, he led the enchantress up onto the weather deck, into the light of the crimson sunset. The Phantom had never seen such a personification of perfection or felt such animal attraction as when he focused on this woman's face. Trying not to look obvious was impossible—he could not take his eyes off her. Standing perfectly situated on her lee, the captain reeled from her fragrance as even the breeze took a gentle turn.

She stood five feet, five inches tall, with thick chestnut locks that framed her exotic features and tumbled down off her shoulders. Her dark brown eyes enhanced her regal elegance. Rosario would soon discover the extraordinary feminine spirit that clung to the lithe and sumptuous body of this enchantress.

Overloaded with booty, Captain Pizzo and the *Blue Dolphin* rejoined the fleet. After looting the *Bernice*, they had set her adrift, leaving her to sail into the legends of ghost ships.

When Pizzo learned of the day's unusual turn of events, he became indignant.

"How could he make such a decision? Nothing good can come of this!"

Because Pizzo was usually a staunch supporter of the Phantom, his first unguarded reaction to hearing about the woman left the rest of his crew unsettled. But despite this brewing discontent, the Phantom's injured fleet, though a little embarrassed at the blunder that had exacted their wounds, hobbled back victoriously toward the Turks Islands, where Rosario anticipated their next visit from Terran.

The Phantom was certain that it would not be much longer before the sky barge was hovering overhead. So far, the Maraudians had always been prompt when it was time to split the booty.

As the *Maraudor* orbited tirelessly above the Earth, there was something that Zalcon found troubling. Unlike Terran, the first mate was concerned that Rosario would recognize the treasure he was taking off the galleon. "If he does realize what's going on," he cautioned, "I doubt he'll continue to go along with us."

It was obvious from Terran's body language that this was of little concern to the space pirate. "There are many fish in the sea," he said, turning to his Atlantic sea charts. "As far as we know, Rosario has already done his best work for us. Now that we have all his treasure, if it becomes necessary, we can cut him loose."

"Agreed, Captain," said Zalcon. "As soon as this business with Lafitte is over, we should immediately focus Rosario on our next mission."

A quick eye-to-eye nod confirmed the captain's agreement on this matter.

Crew members from all three of the Phantom's ships helped man the *Concepción*, which was now second in line behind the *Tortuga Diablo*, with the *Blue Dolphin* and the *Jewel* following closely off the port and starboard sides of their prize.

Sunset found them sailing before a brisk fresh wind, while, back aboard the *Tortuga Diablo*, Rosario brooded about his tenuous arrangement with Terran. As he entered the grand cabin and closed the doors behind him, his concerns about Terran were swept away by a gale force passion, the kind that forges and seasons a sailor's skills, should he survive.

This night on the sea of ecstasy could only be interrupted by the direst of circumstances. Such was the case as the Phantom tore himself away from his bed and listened to what his trusted boatswain was revealing.

"There's trouble in the wind, Cap'n, to be sure," said Knox.

"It's the *Jewel.*"

The Phantom's brotherhood had developed and honed many special skills over the past eleven years. One of these was its highly articulate code, and the ability to scramble any message sent between the buccaneers. Most often, these communications were sent via light flashes from a signal lantern. It was one of these devices that now gave Rosario the advantage of finding out what his partner from space was up to. The steady roll of the inky brine seemed to urge them on as the flashing lights on the *Concepción* revealed the treachery afoot. There was an opinion forming on the galleon that something was amiss in the treasure holds. Rosario's mind raced ahead to the ramifications as the flashing lights repeated the message:

ITEMS FOUND ABOARD FROM BANK OF ROSARIO

No one among the Phantom's staff slept as they sailed all night, making way for Great Inagua Island, planning what action to take. Using their nimble code, they were able to discuss every aspect of the swindle.

It wasn't exactly clear how Lafitte figured in all of this, but it was obvious that the Corsair and Terran were somehow connected. After quelling the crew's first impulse to start shooting the space pirates on sight, Rosario made them understand the futility of such a move and what their strategy must be:

MUST BIDE OUR TIME

NOT LET THEM KNOW WE KNOW
MUST WAIT TO LEARN
THEIR WEAKNESSES
IF WE KEEP OUR HEADS
THEY WILL LOSE THEIRS

The word was passed almost instantly through the four ships.

Even if the Maraudians were directly above, they would not have understood the incessant flashing between the ships as the Phantom and his crew considered their options. In the end, the original strategy still seemed to be the only way to proceed. Rosario's commanders agreed, it would do them no good to object openly to what they knew the Maraudians were doing. Instead, as always, they would play along while they tried to find a way to turn the tables on these rogues.

To say they were spooked was an understatement, but being swindled like this made them more furious than afraid. As the first light began to swallow the night, the closely knit crew members were ready and able to play their part as unsuspecting dunderheads.

The first sight of the space pirates came at daybreak, which was no surprise to Rosario. Always dismayed whenever he saw the terrible Terran, the Phantom wished that somehow something would cause the space captain to disappear. But this recurring fantasy also served to remind him that, so far, he was at a loss to come up with any realistic solution to his quandary.

The Maraudians hovered over the Phantom's fleet as their share of the loot was offloaded. Using three sky barges made the job go faster while imposing on Rosario and his men a deeper sense of inferiority. The hemp gondolas rose and fell many times, extracting the twice stolen treasure under the disciplined and restrained eye of the wily Rosario.

As piece after piece of the opulent cache was lifted, the space pirates were becoming suspicious because Rosario was showing no signs of recognizing his own possessions. Realizing that they were watching him carefully, the Phantom decided to display a small portion of his resentment. As one of two solid gold Pegasus statues was about to move to its new home, he became furious.

"Hold there!" he cried. "Stop the work at once! I recognize that flying horse. It's been stolen from my own secret store." Then, turning to Terran, he exploded, throwing his hands up in the air, "You were supposed to help me *eliminate* the Corsair! Instead, he brings you *my* treasure!"

Rosario's feigned indignation did not phase Terran. Without acknowledging the Phantom's distress, he simply said, "Obviously, Lafitte must have found your hiding place on his own and did what he always does.... But that is not *my* concern. This treasure is now part of a joint mission that we agreed to share evenly. Therefore, I'm well within the terms of our agreement to claim a share."

Terran's words slipped easily from his lips as he smiled confidently.

This proves the man's a ruthless double dealer, thought Rosario. *The Corsair could never have found my hoard without his help. But it would take at least four ships to carry away my treasure. Where's the rest of it?*

Confident that Rosario was still in the dark, Terran fed him another promise of ample compensation. "Never fear, Captain Rosario," he said unctuously, "I can see your point. Be assured that before we're through, your share of our partnership will be many times the amount we have divided thus far."

Rosario only glared at his partner and nodded. The Phantom's humiliating position in this lopsided arrangement was chipping away at his once indelible self-confidence.

By the time Terran's share was offloaded, the long morning was finally over. But then, at midday, the massive galleon took a severe list to port. This startling event ripped Rosario from deep within his own quandary when he learned that the *Concepción*'s crew had left a seacock open before they were forced off the ship. The flooding below decks had gone unnoticed all through the night. By the time it was discovered, the damage was irreparable. Using all hands and working frantically, Rosario barely had time to offload his share of the loot onto the *Tortuga Diablo* before the *Concepción* was gone.

As the Maraudians watched the galleon go down, Zalcon said to Terran, "How are we going to send the *Jewel* into the past, crippled as she is?"

"No problem," said Terran. "After some minor repairs, she'll be like new."

"Will we be able to keep Rosario and his men in the dark about sending them back in time?"

"No," said Terran, "we'll have to tell them what's going on in order for them to carry out our plan. There's no other way."

"So be it," said Zalcon.

It was late morning by the time Rosario was briefed on the next mission.

"You have seen some of the wondrous tools we have," Terran began. "Now you'll see our ability to go back in time. We have a device that will take you back to the world of a hundred years ago. Once there, you will plunder every treasure we can locate."

The matter-of-fact tone in which Terran presented this preposterous concept made it seem plausible. Nevertheless, Rosario didn't like the smell of it.

We'll never survive this, he thought. *Even if they succeed in sending us into the past, who knows if we'll come back in one piece?*

Zalcon handed his captain the chart he was holding.

"Your first target," Terran continued, "will be the *Preciado*. She's a big ship, so there won't be room to offload all of her loot onto the *Jewel*. We'll solve that problem by sinking her in the shallows of Cartan Island..., right *here* on the map. Mandoon will attach a device to her before she goes down, so we will have no trouble locating the treasure upon your return to the present."

This wild plan had Rosario's head spinning, especially since his mind had not cleared since he had met Aleia.

"Our next rendezvous will be in three days," said Terran. "That will give you ample time to make the necessary repairs on the *Jewel*."

Terran marked the coordinates and gave the map to Rosario. The Maraudians then returned to their sky barge.

As the Phantom watched them vanish, he longed for the day they would never return. Each new development with these space pirates increased the constant anxiety he felt in the pit of his stomach.

I wonder if there's any hope of ever returning to the carefree life we once knew.

It was less than a two-day cruise to the coordinates of their next rendezvous, during which Knox would oversee the necessary repairs to the *Jewel*. However, the morale among the Phantom's crew was less than enthusiastic, so Rosario decided to rest his men, waiting until morning to get under way.

"We're in no hurry," he told Rodriquez. "No sense in making an all-night run."

"Yes, Captain," said the first mate. "We could have rendezvoused in two days, but they specified three."

"I wonder what they're up to right now…, and where do they go when they disappear?"

These questions added more fuel to the fires of distrust aboard the *Tortuga Diablo*.

As the crimson sun transformed the blue azure into a blazing backdrop over the troubled fleet, there was a chill in the wind as well as in the mood of the crew. They were backsliding. Losing everything they had pirated over the last eleven years was not what they had had in mind. Rants of discontent rose sporadically among the men as they grappled with their plight.

"Having this woman onboard might be part of the problem," cried one.

"Right!" echoed another. "Things seem to be getting worse since *she's* been with us!"

Rodriquez reported these grumblings of the crew to his captain. But the Phantom wasn't having any. He stormed out of the grand cabin.

"Now, hear this," Rosario announced from the quarterdeck to the crew below, "it's not the woman who's causing our problems, I say. All our troubles come from the terrible Terran. Trust me, we *will* find a way out. Now, get a good night's sleep. We're getting underway at first light."

Although the men took some comfort from their captain's words, the fact that they had broken an ageless taboo by bringing a woman onboard still fed their anxieties.

As the celestial fireball sank below the horizon, Captains Pizzo and Bruno climbed aboard the *Tortuga Diablo* to confer with their commodore, who briefed them on Terran's latest scheme.

"It's madness, Captain," said Pizzo, "to think of going back a hundred years. It's witchcraft."

"We should have it out with them here and now," said Bruno, "and be done with it."

"We have no choice," Rosario said grimly. "Don't you see? If we buck them, they'll send us under for sure! We must wait until something happens that allows us to turn the tables on those space dogs."

"But now that Lafitte has discovered our hideout," said Pizzo, "where are we going to stash what we have aboard?"

"I haven't figured that out yet," Rosario said. "But one thing is certain, I'm not going to let Terran swindle it away, the way he did the rest."

Just before leaving, Pizzo said, "Maybe the answer to all this will come to us in our dreams."

Bruno grumbled, "Aye, it's sleep we need."

When Rosario was alone again, his head was reeling. One after another, these dire circumstances were stacking up in his mind. He knew they would be lucky to escape the Maraudians with their lives.

But then his thoughts returned to the grand cabin and the new fascination waiting within. Normally, Rosario had no trouble organizing his priorities under stress. Up until now, the woman did not exist who could divert him from his duty as a commander of men. The sea had always been his first love, and no painted land lover could ever keep the Phantom's attention more than a night or two. But this woman was beyond anything he had ever come up against. He was swept up in some kind of typhoon of the heart, and was at the storm's mercy. Retiring with Aleia on the *Tortuga Diablo*, he put off the desperate decisions for survival till morning.

In the grand cabin, Rosario and Aleia shared a simple meal of cheese, bread, and wine. They remained in bed until mid-morning activities finally woke the captain from his dreamless coma. The woman slept on as Rosario went out on deck.

The fleet was making for the Turks Islands, where they would rendezvous with the Maraudians and prepare for the next mission.

Rosario was feeling better than he had in months. The brisk sea breeze filled his nostrils, inspiring him with determination to see his way through the maze he was in. While he recalled Terran's description of the simplicities of the next mission, there was a part of him that was working hard to realize the answer to his own treasure problems. It bothered him that Terran did not seem to notice or care that the Phantom needed to stash his share of the loot.

All at once, the answer surfaced in Rosario's crafty consciousness.

I already knew they can't see anything beneath the surface. That's why they need Mandoon's device to find the treasure ship they want us to sink. We still have two more days till the rendezvous..., plenty of time to place our treasure in nets, attach fifty feet of rope to each, and leave them exposed on the weather deck of the Dolphin. Then we'll sink her. When the time is right, we'll haul the goods back up to the surface.

By midday, Rosario's decision was final. The flagship issued orders to the fleet to make for Great Inagua Island. Almost unnoticeable, the variation in course would take the Phantom to some shallows he knew of, off an unnamed outer island. He planned to keep only a token amount of booty aboard the *Tortuga Diablo* and then load the *Blue Dolphin* with the rest of their treasure and sink her there, reporting her as lost in a night storm.

There was some initial resistance on the part of Captain Pizzo and others about sacrificing a perfectly good ship in this way. After further consideration of their predicament and the tremendous value of the booty, however, everyone saw the wisdom in the Phantom's plan.

"It's the only way," Rosario told Pizzo and Bruno. "Terran will never leave without taking everything he can get his greedy hands on."

Although the Phantom was convinced that the Maraudians could see the fleet from above, he felt just as sure that Terran was doing business somewhere else in the world. After being betrayed by Terran's double dealings with Lafitte, he was certain that the space pirate was involved with others as well. This was all speculation, but, regardless, he knew that when the final deal came, it would be treacherous.

By mid-afternoon of the second day, as the Phantom was about to reduce his fleet by one-third, his men watched and waited. Not a word was spoken. Rosario's plan was a drastic and desperate measure. No one wanted to lose the precious *Blue Dolphin*. But, after all was said and done, it was the only way to get by the terrible Terran and his wondrous equipment.

When everything was ready, Rosario gave the command: "Fire!"

The thunder from the three cannons on the *Tortuga Diablo* and the three on the *Jewel* rocked the ships as the order was executed.

It is always a sad occasion to witness the death of a ship, and so it was as the crew watched their treasure-laden friend make the supreme sacrifice for the cause. The *Blue Dolphin* went straight down as a result of six well-placed holes fore and aft below her freeboard.

Silence prevailed as they watched the *Dolphin*'s weather deck slip beneath the waves. Terran's treachery burned white hot within the hearts and minds of the Phantom's men, filling them with a firm resolve. The space pirate had given them a dose of their own medicine, which they resented with every fiber of their being.

Pizzo's crew had been divided among the remaining ships, while he himself was assisting the Phantom aboard the *Tortuga Diablo*. This was not the first time, for Pizzo had been Rosario's first mate once before.

Now only the mastheads of the *Blue Dolphin* were visible. After several large air bubbles boiled to the surface, the water settled again, leaving nothing to indicate what had occurred.

As Rosario set course again for the tiny Turks Islands, the crew continued to fester over Aleia's presence aboard ship. A deckhand could be heard above the other voices. "She may be the cause of our pitiful luck," he lamented, "and now we're in for quite a blow tonight."

As the promised storm continued to close with ever

increasing swells, the crew assembled on the weather deck of the *Tortuga Diablo* and selected James Villa, the third mate, to ask the captain for an audience.

"The men," said Villa, "are troubled about having a woman aboard, Captain, and would have a word with you."

"So be it, then."

As Rosario looked down at the men from the quarterdeck, seeing their love-starved faces somehow warmed his heart. The little embarrassment he felt was indiscernible in the image of confidence he projected.

"I don't want to hear your superstitions and fears concerning the woman," he said.

"But, Captain," shouted an unidentified voice in the crowd, "it's a grievous breach of tradition."

"Aye, Captain," called another, "how can we expect anything good to come of this?"

"It's bad luck, don't ya see?" said a third. "Plain and simple."

"That's where you're wrong," countered Rosario. "If anything, the woman is a *good* omen. The oncoming storm is a sure sign that things are going our way. It's a real piece of good luck…, just what we'll need to convince Terran that the *Blue Dolphin* was truly lost in a storm. I'm sure we'll get our chance to turn things around. Until then, we must hold fast and keep our wits about us. Now, let's hear no more about the woman. The storm is nearly on us, so make ready for high seas."

As the crew prepared for heavy weather, the commander

retired to his quarters and his preoccupation. That they were in for a blow heightened his anticipation of another intimate evening with Aleia.

The timely oncoming storm would indeed provide the perfect backdrop for the story he would tell Terran. Although the storm did not reach gale force, it did impede the ships' nocturnal progress, forcing them to set sea anchors and ride out the violent swells.

At sunrise, the *Tortuga Diablo* and the *Jewel* were striking under clear skies for their rendezvous, none the worse from the storm's fury. They were still two hours out when the sky barge appeared overhead.

When they stepped aboard, Terran and his first officer went directly to the quarterdeck, where Rosario and Pizzo were waiting.

"Where is your *other* ship?" Zalcon demanded, not bothering with formalities.

"The *Dolphin* was compromised below the waterline," Rosario said, without missing a beat. "The storm sealed her fate, and she was lost in the night. We were able to save the crew, but nothing more."

Terran and Zalcon exchanged glances, but seemed satisfied with this story.

"We've decided to modify our plan," Terran said. "To ensure your success, we're going to install a second sonic cannon on the *Jewel*."

"Why do we need a second cannon?" Pizzo asked.

Zalcon's cliché retort denoted a certain impatience.

"Two cannons," he said, "are better than one."

Rosario simply nodded, but said nothing. *Maybe,* he thought, *this is the opportunity we've been waiting for..., if we can turn their own guns against them.*

For the rest of that day, while the additional sonic cannon was installed on the *Jewel's* stern, Lieutenant Zane and Will Knox, using the first cannon, trained a second team to fire it.

The following morning, Mandoon arrived with the time portal, which by midday he had secured snugly on deck, exactly amidships. He remained hunched over the controls, mumbling and adjusting the flashing panel on the side of the triangular device until he seemed satisfied that everything was in order.

Zalcon and Zane looked on as the two gun crews practiced the procedures over and over. Knox would not let them make the same mistake that he had made on his first run, so they practiced the rest of the remaining daylight hours.

That night, aboard the *Maraudor,* Terran, Zalcon, and Mandoon carefully checked the charts against the reports in the Gazetteer. Choosing the narrow sea lane between Santo Domingo and Puerto Rico, they would lie in wait a few miles northeast of the Puerto Rican Trench.

When they had finalized their intrepid plan, Mandoon announced some progress in achieving a stress-free transition for the time travelers.

"Something to do with direction and seamless reentry," he said.

Terran was not impressed. "You'll have to do better than that," he said. "Keep on it. I'm sure I don't have to tell *you* the importance of getting it right."

Terran's words dashed the faint flicker of hope within the wizard for the approval he had been craving from his captain. Instead, all he could think was, *He's willing to gamble my life to learn the secrets of this infernal device.*

In a less pointed tone, Terran added, "It seems you're on the verge of a breakthrough. I have every confidence that you will find your answers by the time you return."

Backhanded as this was, Terran's encouraging remark felt like redemption to a scolded poodle. "Thank you, Captain."

Zalcon actually felt a flash of pity for the wizard. Mandoon's short but sincere answer struck both officers as a sign of his waning self-confidence.

Meanwhile, on the *Tortuga Diablo*, Rosario was indisposed. The lovestruck captain had scarcely been seen the whole week. Aleia was also never seen. If she came outside at all, it was only after dark. Rosario had left the preparations and training to the others as he lingered as long as possible in the throes of his passionate obsession.

Rosario was basking in the golden rapture he felt from loving this woman. It occurred to him that although his vast treasure trove had been swindled away, the loss was a numb background twinge, hardly noticeable in contrast to the warm delectable slice of life that was his new treasure.

Early in the morning on the day before the time mission, Terran, Mandoon, and Zalcon stepped aboard the *Tortuga Diablo* for a final briefing with Rosario and his officers. While Knox waited with the Maraudians, Captain Pizzo knocked on the door of the grand cabin to summon Rosario to the business at hand. When he knocked a second time, the door opened.

Captain Pizzo may have been many things, but in the presence of Aleia he was but a man. When their eyes met, neither one was ready for the shock. Aleia not only felt the deep attraction that swept through Pizzo in a flash, but his heartbeat quickened her own.

"Captain Pizzo, ma'am," he said at last. "I'm here for Captain Rosario. He's needed at the meeting for tomorrow's mission."

Pizzo had said the magic word as far as she was concerned— *captain.*

Aleia smiled as she put her finger to her lips impishly. "He still sleeps," she said softly. Then, pushing Pizzo back, she stepped outside, closing the cabin door behind her. She could have pushed Pizzo overboard. He was defenseless—and she knew it. He was swept away. Like all the rest, another captain had come to her. He stood before her, smitten and powerless to deflect any whim she might dictate.

Aleia focused on Pizzo with an alluring smile. This man was more than just the next captain she would seduce. She felt a hot flush of excitement streak through her body that was unlike anything she had ever experienced before.

Every preconception about Rosario's woman evaporated

from Pizzo's mind as obsession seized him. He was struck silent in a warm, fuzzy cloud of spontaneous passion that raced his pulse and reddened his face. There was lightning in the connection when their eyes met. Aleia felt it and recognized the extraordinary feeling as her first opportunity for real contentment.

On her own since her early teens, Aleia had come from gypsies. Her stunning beauty had made her as much of a victim as any of the men she loved and left. She had become used to being at sea, snug and secure as the captain's woman. Early on, her mother had told her she would never settle long anywhere when she sold her daughter to a traveling circus.

"You have the wind in your hair, learn to embrace it," was her mother's parting advice.

Circus life was much more colorful than her time with the gypsies, and the very young Aleia welcomed the change. Her circus family was a close-knit collection of skills, talents, and Bohemian customs. Always receiving kind and fair treatment from these people, she quickly adopted them as her own. In those years before her first sea captain, they taught her their many insights into human nature, secrets that could be relied on to produce any desired result. Aleia internalized these lessons with an ease that often astounded her benefactors.

She was quick to discover the power she held over men and her natural ability to apply it. Her enchanting visage had a stunning effect that allowed her to control any man she met. Prewarned, perhaps, a wise man would have had her banished in chains if this were the only way to retain his freedom. Instead, freedom seemed like a worthless trinket to the men who fell prey to her. Over the last five years, she had been with six captains and knew well how to manipulate them.

Now, as the wind blew gently outside the grand cabin, Aleia liked what she saw — Pizzo's potential as her next steppingstone. After an intensive five days of love Rosario-style, she knew a change was inevitable, if not already at hand.

"If you are a captain," she whispered, "then take me with you, for I am a captain's woman."

Unleashing herself like this swept Pizzo out of his world of reason, throwing him into a swimming struggle for composure. The delicious creature wrapped around the tall sailor and locked her lips to his.

Grappling with his sense of duty and reason, Pizzo broke free from her passionate embrace, just managing to put a couple of feet between Aleia and himself, when the door swung open and Rosario stepped out, still a bit groggy. It was Pizzo's good fortune that the door had not opened one second earlier. If it had, blood would have spilled. As it was, the sleepy captain did not have a clue.

Pizzo stammered, "It's...uh...Terran and his mates, Captain. They're waiting for you on the quarterdeck." A twinge of guilt could be heard in his voice, but went unnoticed by Rosario, while Aleia slipped inside, continuing to stare at Pizzo intensely from over Rosario's shoulder.

Pizzo pretended not to notice.

"I'll be there presently," Rosario said, turning back into his state room.

"Aye, Captain," Pizzo said, looking over Rosario's back, nodding and smiling tenderly to the coquette. His eyes never left hers as Rosario kicked the door shut behind him.

Pizzo seemed to stagger as he returned to the quarterdeck, preoccupied with a plan that was already forming in his brain. Noticing that the Maraudians and Knox were staring at him with curiosity, he blurted out what they were waiting to hear: "The captain will be here presently."

Everyone on the quarterdeck waited in silence as the ship rolled gently over the morning swells. Warm spring weather came early in these southern seas, changing the morose grey canopy into a jubilant blue backdrop, with towering white thunderheads above endless aqua swells rolling in search of land.

These exotic conditions always had the same effect on the crew, but this spring was different. Since their recent alliance with the pirates of Marauda, all thoughts of carefree liberties on shore were out of the question. Lately, there was no time for anything but the Maraudians' agenda. This year their spring fever raged only in their memories. They were no longer free to blow with the wind.

When the Phantom appeared on the quarterdeck, he looked well rested. Terran did not indicate the surprise he felt at Rosario's high spirits as they went over the final details of their scheme.

"You and Captain Bruno," Terran said to Rosario, "will take the *Jewel* on the mission while Captain Pizzo stays behind to command the *Tortuga Diablo*."

"The woman comes with me," Rosario insisted.

"Totally out of the question," said Terran. "This is a Marau-dian mission, and there will be no women involved."

Rosario clenched his teeth and silently cursed Terran, but said no more for the moment.

"As I was about to say," Terran continued, "as soon as you have secured the prize, you will sail the *Jewel* to the coordinates supplied to you at that time by Mandoon, taking the *Preciado* with you. After you offload all the gold onto the *Jewel* that she can carry, you will sink the *Preciado* with the remaining booty. Then Mandoon will activate the time portal to bring you all back here."

Rosario returned to his quarters as soon as the meeting con-cluded, unaware that things had changed for Aleia. She would go along with her present arrangement one more night so as not to disturb Rosario before he left on the mission. There would be plenty of time to deal with his disappointment once she had made the next move in her insatiable quest.

Commander Zalcon was right about maximizing Mandoon's focus on the time portal's problems by assigning him to the mis-sion. Mandoon was spending all his time on the *Jewel*, trying to solve the problem of the potential for cerebral abrasions when using the time device. Although Terran had no other choice but to gamble Mandoon in this way, he maintained his usual façade of dispassionate concern. As the time to disembark drew near, the science officer felt he was on the verge of a breakthrough.

"The problem has something to do with alignment and reentry," he told his captain. "I will instruct the crew to stand in the same place and position, keeping their eyes fixed, during both our entry into the past and our return back to the present."

Mandoon was a skillful scientist, who tested his hypotheses systematically, recording a comprehensive description of every aspect of the experiment.

"As we reenter this temporal zone," he said, "we must meet our point of origin seamlessly. That is, when we arrive back here, we need to be standing very close to the same position, facing in the same direction as when we left. The abrasions occur when these conditions do not prevail. Failure to take these precautions will cause the central nervous system to mismatch with itself, resulting in incoherence, at the very least."

Terran and Zalcon listened to the commander's hypothesis, remaining silent for several moments after hearing his fantastic interpretations.

"As usual," the captain finally replied, "it would seem your performance under pressure has enabled us to succeed. Well done, Commander. I'm sure you're on the right track, and under your guidance the mission will be a complete success." Terran's response was meant to let Mandoon's optimism surge.

Zalcon knew the captain had exaggerated in his attempt to inflate Mandoon to maximum performance. Mandoon, on the other hand, lapped up each kind word like drops of water in the desert.

To fortify their chance of success, Terran had directed Rosario to take along every available crewman.

Despite his strong desire to the contrary, Rosario agreed to leave Aleia behind, out of harm's way, for the anticipated three- or four-day mission. Captain Pizzo, whom he trusted like a brother, would temporarily command the *Tortuga Diablo* with a skeleton crew, along with the cabin boy and the captain's woman. All other sailors would be aboard the timeship, a complement of two hundred and forty souls, the largest crew ever assembled on the *Jewel*. Rosario would not dash the hopes of his high-spirited men with his gloomy version of their predicament.

As the morning sun appeared on the horizon, the sky barge hovered above to pick up Terran and Zalcon. With the departure of the *Jewel* only moments away, Rosario and his officers elected not to burden the crew with the fact that they would be traveling through time.

As always, Zalcon concealed his movements as he made some last-minute adjustments to the sonic cannons. Then, turning to Mandoon, he said, "The guns will remain active for approximately sixty hours. That should be all the time you'll need. Do you know the formula to reactivate them if necessary?"

Mandoon snapped back with a tone of impatience meant to extinguish Zalcon's negative opinion. "Of *course*, I do!"

Mandoon had told them that the transition back into the past would be unnoticeable out at sea. Shortly after the sky barge departed, the *Jewel* got under way toward Mandoon's coordinates. It would take all day and all night to reach the point over the Puerto Rican Trench where they anticipated intercepting the *Preciado* and her escorts, the *Prince* and the *Ortega*.

II

A brisk wind made for perfect conditions as they ran south under a searing sun and cloudless azure. Mandoon had Knox assemble the crew amidships, where the science officer tried to explain that they must stand in the same spot when they disembarked and when they returned. Only the officers understood what he was so awkwardly describing to the men. Zalcon's explanation at their briefing had been much easier to understand. Both versions were vague at best and failed to mention the potential for dire consequences.

The night sky, replete with every visible citizen of the Milky Way, promised a fair cruise into tomorrow.

Rosario was feeling the terrible void that intensified with each passing hour. He had been born to the sway of the sea, but, for the first time, the constant creaking noises were attached to his aching heart, or so it seemed, as the pangs of Aleia's absence tormented his sleepless night. He had no way of knowing that he was only another rung on an endless ladder, and had already served the purpose of the untamable temptress.

Two weeks prior, he never would have believed that he could be so hopelessly obsessed with a woman. In the short string of days since finding her, his whole world had been in flux, as he constantly pushed daily priorities aside to stay with her. Now all that really mattered was getting back to her. This meant more than getting even with Terran, but he would still try to accomplish both, and the sooner the better.

I know the day will come when only one of us will survive.

In his characteristic style, the Phantom waited at sunrise at the coordinates, ready to strike at first sight of the expected prey. To get the crew on deck, he shouted to the drummer, "Beat to quarters!"

When everyone was present, Mandoon once again addressed the crew. "Men," he began, "take note of where you are standing at this moment, facing the bow, and don't move until I tell you. When we return from our mission, you must be in exactly the same position you are in now."

After some confusion, the crew seemed to get the idea. They stood braced with eyes looking forward.

Positioned at the triangular device, Mandoon moved his hand over the glowing side panel. A blinding white light cracked and flashed, turning everything for a split second as bright as the center of the sun.

In that instant, the contentment of that warm, clear morning was abruptly transformed into a dense overcast canopy, replete with green-lined thunderheads boiling into towering giants that threatened a deluge.

Once again Mandoon addressed the crew: "It is done. You are now free to move about." Then, pointing straight ahead, he said to Rosario, "Look! There on the horizon!"

When everyone turned, they saw what they had come for. There were three silhouettes running before the wind, where only a moment before, there were none.

Mandoon was animated. He stood beaming beside the time portal, validated in his ability.

As soon as the *Jewel* appeared, the frigates altered course to intercept.

The Phantom immediately hoisted the colors of Spain, hoping his old trick would not fail him against these aggressive warships.

Mandoon stood beside Rosario as the captain prepared for battle.

"If nothing else," Rosario explained, "the colors will cause them to think twice before shooting."

Mandoon smiled as he began to understand the Phantom's tactic. The *Jewel* continued on course as the frigates bore down.

In little more than a week, the six carpenters from the Phantom's fleet had performed an excellent refitting of the *Jewel*. She had always been the fastest of Rosario's fleet, and the eighty feet of white waterline that marked her way confirmed that her agility was unimpaired.

The rapidly forming thunderheads indicated that a cloudburst was imminent.

Looking skyward, Rosario grimaced. "I only hope," he said, "we can take care of business before this squall cuts loose."

Regardless, they had made their play and were well past the point of no return. The galleon made a dash, taking full advantage of running before the wind. The lead frigate, the *Ortega*, would have to be dealt with before going after the prize. The second frigate, the *Prince*, was off the treasure galleon's starboard when the Phantom appeared, and would consequently be a little late when the shooting started.

As the *Preciado* desperately lumbered off, the *Ortega* was almost in range. Normally at this point, cannons should have commenced firing. The fact that they had not made Rosario grin, knowing that his flag trick had worked as he gripped his cutlass and intensified his focus on the *Ortega*.

"At least, they're not shooting," he said to Mandoon.

Rosario would wait to get as close to the *Prince* as he could. With squinted eyes, he spoke softly to his opponents, as if they were as close to him as Mandoon.

"That's it, a little more, yes, that's it."

Rosario would never know what finally tipped off the *Ortega*. She suddenly swerved to starboard and brought all guns to bear. That was enough for the Phantom. "Fire at will!" he cried.

Knox responded immediately with a double burst to the great main mast. The quick succession snapped the mighty teak spar like a dry twig, and it came crashing down. The crew collapsed, never knowing what hit them. By the time the rigging had fallen on the decks and into the sea, the *Jewel* was passing her on her way toward the *Preciado*. Mandoon pointed out that the stricken frigate could still pose a threat if the crew were to revive in time to come to the aid of the quarry.

Without a second thought, Rosario turned to Bruno's crew. "Stand by on the aft cannon!"

"Manned and ready, Captain!" came Bruno's instant response.

The oncoming storm rocked the haggard *Ortega* over the steadily building swells. Captain Bruno and his aft cannon crew stood ready, eager to hear the word. Aboard the listing *Ortega*, her motionless crew would never know what hit them.

"Fire!" Rosario ordered, sending a second barrage to make sure he would not be hindered any further.

Captain Bruno responded with another double dose of the lethal sound blasts. It was Bruno's first hard target since he had completed his training. His aim was a little low. The frigate would soon succumb to Bruno's hull-bursting low shot, which had also killed the entire crew. In the heat of the moment, no one noticed that the fatal damage was the result of bad aim. There was too much going on to look back.

The *Prince* was striking desperately to engage the *Jewel* to prevent her from continuing in hot pursuit of the *Preciado*. After an hour, the stage was set once again for the next engagement. Realizing that escape was futile, the captain of the *Preciado* turned into the wind. Opening the doors of her twenty-five port-side cannons, the ship let loose with a thunderous fusillade.

The captains of the *Prince* and the *Preciado* believed that they had the Phantom bracketed. The massive treasure galleon housed cannons on three decks. Her hull seemed to be incredibly thick and impenetrable. As he watched the great ship making her last desperate move, Rosario was thankful he wasn't depending on conventional firepower, for he knew that a devastating wall of hot steel was about to be unleashed at him. This time, he would not wait a second longer than was necessary to ensure obliteration.

"Fire at will as they come to bear!" he ordered.

In another moment, it would begin. The *Prince* would have to wait a little longer to make the reach.

"Mind you don't sink her..., aim high!"

Rosario's last piece of advice fell on deaf ears as both gun crews focused on their targets. It was a tight situation. Even with the advantage of the space weapons, things could get out of hand if either ship were able to get off a barrage.

Rosario came hard to port for his firing position. As the *Jewel* came around, the *Prince*, now barely in range, fired all her cannons. The Phantom swung hard over, skillfully dodging most of the *Prince*'s desperate long shot. A half-dozen cannonballs tore through the sails on the aft mast, while another crashed through the quarterdeck. Although moderately damaged, the *Jewel* did not miss a beat.

Before the *Prince* could get off another round, Will Knox sent a triple sound blast smashing into the galleon, bursting masts and neutralizing her crew. A great wave of relief came over the

Phantom at being spared for another chance at success.

Captain Bruno did not need Rosario to give him the word this time. He fired on the *Prince* as soon as he had the shot. Squeezing the trigger device repeatedly, Bruno reduced the frigate into flotsam amidst flame-less explosions and splintering wood.

There followed a relative silence as bodies and rubble rode the rolling swells under ever-darkening midday skies. This vicious second round was over in minutes.

Among the devastated fleet, only the great treasure galleon was not in immediate danger of sinking. The *Prince* was already gone, and the *Ortega* would sink before long.

Rosario brought the *Jewel* alongside the *Preciado* on her port side because her starboard was strewn with spars, sails, and rigging, the upper half of the main mast hopelessly tangled and clinging to her.

Grappling hooks pulled the *Preciado* into the *Jewel*'s clutches as the first of the Phantom's men boarded the fallen galleon to get her ready to sail, normally a chore that was made effortless by the thrill of the hunt and winning the prize. On this occasion, Rosario was in a bind. No longer were he and his men buccaneers, free and clear. They had become henchmen for the terrible Terran of Marauda. Rosario knew he must bide his time and wait for the chance to turn the tables. But it was disheartening that no opportunities had yet presented themselves, and he was at a loss for ideas.

As if to accent his despair, jagged silver fingers of lightning pierced the pea-green sky.

Instinctively, Rosario waited for the thunder, but none came.

All this treasure was only an obstacle to him now, keeping him away from his Aleia.

If I ever get back with her, I'll find a way to resolve this predicament with Terran.

Suddenly, Rosario was ripped from his obsession by a blast from reality.

Kaboom! Boom! Boom!

The *Preciado* was not licked yet. Three of the central cannons on her third deck were still in commission, as was made apparent by the three holes smashed through the *Jewel's* freeboard. Fortunately, the two ships were too close to allow the *Preciado* a shot below the waterline.

Everyone was caught off guard. The first response came from Bruno, who, without adjusting the cannon's angle, let loose with successions of sonic blasts, impacting the *Preciado* above and below the waterline. The resulting gaping holes immediately flooded the treasure-laden galleon, hopelessly condemning her to the abominable depths of the Puerto Rican Trench.

The massive ship was sinking fast. There was barely time to rescue the Phantom's men, who were stunned by Bruno's barrage. Cries of awe and surprise rang out from the crew as they watched the *Preciado* being swallowed whole by the boiling sea, never to be seen again.

A single wrenching cry followed as Mandoon realized what had just occurred. It was a gruesome, terrorized shriek of despair. He anticipated the ultimate blame, punishment, and scorn that Terran would issue, along with his unimaginable wrath. What could he tell his captain that would stave off his livid disappointment?

As Rosario's mind cleared, he quickly assessed what had just occurred and its ramifications: the mission was a complete failure. This was similar to the incident on the *Concepción*, because the space cannon was not as effective below the second decks of these huge treasure galleons. Rosario made a mental note of this as he turned to ask Mandoon about going back. One look at the distraught space wizard told him that the man was incommunicado.

Mandoon was beside himself with the thought of reporting back to Terran.

He'll terminate me then and there. There's nothing left to say..., I'm finished.

Closing his eyes, Mandoon shrank to the base of the portal.

In an effort to console him, Rosario said, "I'll tell Terran how you weren't to blame, how the situation got out of hand."

But his words had no effect as Mandoon retreated deep within himself.

As long as he remains like this, Rosario thought, *we'll be trapped in the past. He's the only one who knows how to bring us back home again.*

It was midday. The storm could wait no longer. While the catatonic wizard fell into the depths of despair, lightning and thunder exploded the sky, setting off the anticipated deluge.

A driving rain fell relentlessly all through the night, but damage control efforts succeeded in keeping the *Jewel* afloat. Just before first light, the storm had one last tantrum before giving way to a spectacular sunrise and clear skies. Gentle breezes prevailed while Rosario and his men rested from their ordeal. By midday, repairs to the holes in the freeboard and the torn rigging were under way.

But morale was low, for the word was out among the crew that they were trapped in time. The thought that they were dependent on the paralyzed Mandoon plunged them all into the depths of gloom.

Mandoon's condition had not changed at all. He sat on the deck with his eyes closed, not speaking, but accepting the food he was given. Rosario decided to give him some time to get a grip on himself while the crew got a day's rest and recuperation. The hours slipped by as the rolling swells provided some semblance of motion to the listless *Jewel*.

The recent turn of events had extinguished the last remnants of Rosario's optimism. He was engrossed with trying to see his way out of this unbelievable situation. So long as the Maraudians were on the scene, his life as a buccaneer was over. When he was not thinking about how to bring Mandoon around, he was obsessed with finding a way to hide with Aleia until the Maraudians went back to wherever they had come from. He no longer believed it was possible to recoup all the treasure he had lost. With each new mission, losing everything seemed more likely, as things just kept getting worse.

After sunset, Rosario, Bruno, and Knox went to check on Mandoon, who was sitting semi-catatonic at the base of the time portal, never leaving his spot except for a few necessary trips to the leeside of the ship. There he had remained, hour after hour, unwilling to interact with anyone or anything except his meals when they arrived.

Failing in their attempts to make Mandoon respond, the others left him with a blanket.

"I'll deal with him tomorrow," said Rosario. "Good night, gentlemen."

Ready for sleep, the Phantom went to his quarters, leaving Mandoon alone on the deck.

The thought of Terran's wrath kept the science officer terrified.

Losing a treasure haul is a blunder that Terran will not readily forgive. If he spares me, my life will be miserable at best. I have no idea what I can do, but until I come up with a solution, I'm not going back.

Before the ship finally quieted down for the night, an irate rumbling from the crew rose above the normal sounds of the evening.

When Rosario awoke the next morning, he heard some of the crew shouting, obviously at Mandoon.

"Take us back, you madman!"

"Aye, before we do something we all regret!"

"We're in the hands of a coward, lads!"

With his energy now restored, Rosario declared to himself,

"This has gone far enough!" He threw some water on his face and rushed down to the weather deck. As he made his way, he thought to himself, *Another day, another step toward hell!*

Frustration was plunging the crew into a depression that would soon be as perilous as a hull breach. Rosario knew that unless he could snap Mandoon back into cooperating, their situation would quickly deteriorate beyond redress.

The science officer was about to receive his breakfast when Rosario appeared.

"Hold on! There'll be no breakfast for him till he takes us back."

Mandoon's face twitched several times, but he made no other response.

By midday, a second meal was brought to the space wizard, but Rosario once again ordered it withheld.

This time, Mandoon stirred. "If you starve me," he said, "you will *never* be able to return!"

Captain Bruno was quick to respond. "We won't starve you to death," he said, "only enough for you to change your hopeless behavior and put us back on course. We can't stay in this place day after day. Only by returning can we hope to find solutions to our problems."

A chorus of gruff encouragement followed Bruno's eloquence as the *Jewel* pitched and rolled away its time in Limbo.

In the greed-driven culture of the Maraudians, hunger was a condition they found unbearable. Rosario noted this obvious weakness when, after missing only one meal, Mandoon was willing to break his silence. He and Bruno worked on the man together.

"Mandoon," said Rosario, "I give you my word that I will tell Terran that the failed mission was in no way your fault."

"That's right," said Bruno. "It was *my* fault. I fired the shot that sank the prize..., and I will tell your captain as much."

Mandoon listened, seeming to consider their words, but remained reluctant. The Phantom did not know, and Mandoon did not tell him, about the mind reading Hat. Terran did not need to listen to any defense that Rosario could mount on the wizard's behalf. Once the Maraudians had Mandoon back on the mother ship, they would simply put the Hat on his head to discover the truth about everything that had transpired.

Suddenly, the lookout broke the late morning drudgery with a call to action, "Sails ho!"

"What now?" cried Rosario, jumping to his feet. "Where away?"

"Three points off the larboard bow, Captain," cried the look-out.

Knox handed Rosario his fine telescope. The Phantom could plainly see one royal sloop and two smaller ones bearing down on the *Jewel*. Taking advantage of the wind contributed to the considerable speed of their approach.

"They've got the weather gage, Cap'n," said Knox, "and they'll be upon us in no time."

"Beat to quarters!" Rosario ordered. "Make all guns ready! And reef the sails for battle! Arm yourselves to the teeth, men, and prepare to fight or die!"

It was evident to the wily Phantom that these ships were expecting an engagement, probably with the *Preciado* and her escorts.

With less than an hour until they would be in range, Knox and his gun crew manned the forward sonic cannon. But it soon became obvious that things were not right with the sonic blasters, since both gun captains reported no response when they attempted to activate the intensity settings. The familiar vibrating hum was absent, and there was no other indication that they were operational.

When Rosario reported the problem to Mandoon, the science officer said, "The guns need to be reset with an updated code before they will come on line. It's a safety feature meant to keep an enemy from commandeering and using the weapon. The formula for determining the correct sequence will take some time to calculate."

Now, as Rosario looked back at the oncoming royal sloop with his fine telescope, he could read her name as clearly as the crew would in another quarter hour. Running with the wind was an easy trick for the nimble sloop as she cut through the afternoon swells. While he watched, all three ships hoisted confirmation to the Phantom's suspicions—the legendary ensigns were those of none other than the most infamous of sea robbers ever to plague the shipping lanes of the Atlantic and Caribbean.

They were back in the golden age of pirates, caught by surprise and outnumbered. A cry of desperate anticipation rose up from the crew when the black flag unfurled, revealing a horned skeleton holding a pitchfork in one hand and an empty hourglass in the other. They knew its message well — that their hour with the devil was at hand, and the devil was none other than the notorious Edward Teach, alias Blackbeard!

Rosario was all too familiar with the legends and reputation of the most dreaded of all black-hearted pirates. The Jolly Roger was Blackbeard's offer to allow them to surrender and be spared without a fight.

But Rosario would not yield to this master of psychological warfare. Believing that his superior firepower would prevail, he gave his men brace with words of encouragement. "Even Blackbeard," he shouted, "won't be able to withstand the surprise we have for him!"

Turning to Mandoon, Rosario demanded an immediate resolution to the problem. "Be quick or be dead!" he said. "One way or another, if you don't get them armed and ready, you'll not survive the hour!"

As Mandoon ran to the forward gun, he realized that it was too late to activate the time portal, for the crew was spread all over the ship. He was unaware of the sea devil's reputation as he endeavored to bring the forward cannon on line.

The largest of the three sloops came into range on the *Jewel*'s port side, confirming to one and all that she was the infamous *Queen Anne's Revenge*. Now there could be no doubt, they were indeed about to engage Blackbeard and his band of blackguards.

It was a brisk morning wind that enabled the three sloops to come in so efficiently. As the *Queen Anne's Revenge* closed the last hundred yards, the winds diminished to nothing, slowing her momentum, but not her intent.

Realizing Blackbeard meant to attack from both sides, Rosario ran out both the starboard and portside batteries with orders to fire as the enemy came to bear.

Mandoon was having difficulty. His movements over the control panel were becoming more frantic as he repeated the sequence that should have brought the space cannon to life.

Knox watched his every move, becoming familiar with what had been, up until now, a secret procedure.

"What's wrong?" he demanded of the science officer. "Why can't we shoot?"

The only answer was the panic-stricken expression on Mandoon's tormented face as his eyes met Knox's. Then, returning to the glowing buttons, he continued punching at them with one sequence after another.

The Phantom's men were familiar with the legendary tales of Blackbeard and the *Queen Anne's Revenge*. She was formerly the *Concorde*, a European merchant ship, British-built with a Dutch fluyt style, which Blackbeard had captured and made his flagship, increasing the number of her cannons from thirty-two to forty.

As soon as the royal sloop came about, Blackbeard unleashed his first barrage. The specialized personnel salvo had a shorter range than the eighteen-pound hull busters. He wanted to reduce his opposition, not sink the ship.

"Everybody down, down on the deck!" Rosario ordered, just before the vicious barrage of grapeshot tore and splintered everything as it raked three feet above the weather deck of the *Jewel*. There were more than a few men who did not escape the twenty-gun assault. Rosario responded with both chain shot and grapeshot, showering the *Queen Anne's* weather deck and tearing at her rigging.

The gun crews on both ships scrambled desperately to reload for another attempt, as Blackbeard's number two ship, the *Adventure*, came into position, raking the Phantom's stern with both grapeshot and exploding ball shot. The *Jewel* was defenseless as its rudder disintegrated and fell away.

The smallest of the three sloops, the *Revenge*, came along Rosario's starboard side and delivered another grapeshot barrage from her eight cannons. The *Jewel*'s starboard battery let fly at the same instant. Although the *Jewel* sustained further damage, the *Revenge* took the full brunt of the *Jewel*'s guns, causing her to break off her attack and lumber out of range to lick her wounds.

Seeing the *Revenge* disengage, Rosario shouted out, "Fight harder, men! Now there are only two of them!"

In the midst of the pandemonium, a cheer from the Phantom's crew rose above the din. Once again, their captain's words had summoned their courage and confidence.

All this time, Mandoon kept punching away at the sonic cannon, thoroughly perplexed, as Knox and the gun crew hugged the deck.

Before Blackbeard got his chance, Rosario cut loose with a second flock of destruction to the aft section of the *Queen Anne's Revenge*. Once again, Blackbeard's cannons sprayed the *Jewel* with grapeshot as Rosario's men hit the deck. The *Adventure* came around and delivered another salvo to the *Jewel*'s stern, fatally wounding Bruno and his gun crew, as well as destroying the aft sonic cannon. Even heavily damaged, Blackbeard's voracious fleet made short work of disabling the *Jewel*.

Realizing the horrific damage sustained by the *Jewel* had left them dead in the water, Rosario ordered all his men below decks. He would try to make it seem worse than it was and take his chances at close combat when the sea robbers came onboard.

He didn't have long to wait.

As the *Jewel* drifted in the wind, the sloops came alongside port and starboard, letting their grappling hooks fly. As soon as they were in position, the crews of both sloops tossed grenades. Immediately following the explosions, the boarding began. Undaunted, and not knowing that they were outnumbered, Blackbeard's men came pouring over the side amidst rabid battle cries, jeers, and gestures.

Rosario watched from his hiding place as they swung over and leaped from boarding planks. The first one to stand on the decks of the faltering *Jewel* was none other than Blackbeard himself. Presenting a most nefarious image, he stood towering above all the others amidst bloodthirsty threats, sporadic pistol shots, and flailing axes and cutlasses. He was hissing through his teeth words that had been taught to him by Satan. His battle dress included smoldering slow fuses that dangled from the midnight coils of his hair, with black ribbons streaming from his braided beard. He was armed with crisscrossing bandoliers stuffed with daggers and no less than six pistols.

The blackguards' banter quieted smartly when they could not find any live opposition.

Rosario quietly passed the order to his anxious crew to wait for the word. With over thirty bodies lying about the weather deck, he hoped that Blackbeard's men would think that the ship was helpless. As the enemy began to relax, ready to believe their job was done, the Phantom and his crew sprang wildly from all sides, and the final battle ensued in earnest.

The element of surprise gave Rosario's men some advantage, which they made the most of. More than a few of Blackbeard's men fell almost instantly as they were attacked from every direction. The fighting raged on throughout the ship. Rosario was wounded when he and Blackbeard faced off. The Phantom engaged Blackbeard first with pistols. Blackbeard fired first, but somehow missed. Rosario's shot did not, but the raging black giant never faltered as he slashed away at Rosario and several others within his reach. Flames and pistols flickered everywhere before the fighting settled into swinging cutlasses.

On and on, the two oversized crews clashed, as men fell dead or dying on both sides. At one point, Blackbeard snapped Rosario's sword in half with one of his vicious swipes. The blackest of all buccaneers was every bit the swashbuckler that legend had reported him to be, as he sustained wound after wound, including several more pistol shots. Never ceasing his bellowing battle cries, he slashed away at Rosario. The Phantom had no idea how the general battle was going. He could only hope his men were doing better as a whole than he was personally. He could not tell from his quick glances of the bodies that covered the decks as he continued to take on the fighting dynamo.

At one point, Knox, who had been defending Mandoon as he cowered behind the furiously flailing boatswain, saw his chance. Running up behind Blackbeard, he slashed his throat. Even then, as his blood ran yet another tributary to the red river flowing on the deck, the inhuman blackguard continued to fight in a raging fury. Finally, in the midst of cocking his last loaded pistol, the grizzly giant fell dead at Rosario's feet. Exhilaration shot through Rosario. He no longer felt his wounds as he looked to see if anyone else had witnessed the tyrant fall.

Word passed like lightning from those who saw him go down. Upon hearing their captain was gone, all of his men who were able quit the fight and scrambled back aboard their ships. Some were forced to leap off the stern or the bow and swim for it.

Rosario's wounds were bloody, but not life-threatening. As he got to his feet, he struggled to clear the fog in his head. The decks of the *Jewel* were strewn with dead and wounded. In the water, Blackbeard's men were in full retreat. While those who could scurried back to their ships, those who could not were the first to reach that place where they would all end up before this day was over.

Priorities flooded back through Rosario's battle shock. "The time portal!" he yelled, as he swung around to see, amidst the splintered decks and torn rigging, that the triangular device was intact, apparently unscathed.

"Looks undamaged from 'ere, Cap'n," said Knox.

Rosario turned to see his faithful boatswain standing over Blackbeard's body. In one hand, he held the marvelous cutlass that did the deed, and in the other, the trembling Mandoon.

Glaring at the twitching mass of miscalculations, Rosario growled, "I trust you'll be ready to take us back *now*!"

Mandoon had reached his limit. Thoroughly humiliated, the terrified magus nodded submissively.

Rosario could see that Mandoon was on the verge of coming apart. The sound of axes meant that the pirates on both sloops were trying to put this day behind them as, one after another, the lines of the grappling hooks were severed. Both of Blackbeard's crews had shrunk to below the minimum number needed to sail their damaged ships. Clearly, they would be leaving at a much slower pace than when they came calling. Still in a rage, wanting more fight, the Phantom's men jeered the pirates as they sought to disengage.

Pizzo's boatswain, James Villa, wanted to finish them once and for all. "Shall we man the cannons, sir?" he asked.

"Let them go!" Rosario snapped back. "We have our own concerns!"

His only thought now was to get back to Aleia. Turning to Knox, he said, "Clear the decks and throw all the dead and any wounded pirates overboard."

"At once, Cap'n!" said Knox. Then, relaying the order, he cried, "Alright, mates, we're goin' 'ome! Clear the decks. Wounded pirates and all the dead over the side!"

The men on the quarterdeck were already carrying out the orders even as Knox spoke.

Looking around, Rosario saw that most of his crew had survived the battle. Nevertheless, the Phantom had suffered a painful share of fallen crew members, chief among whom was the *Jewel's* Captain Bruno.

Rosario's head began to spin as he thought of what was happening. Not only had he traveled back in time, but he had fought and defeated the most infamous of all pirates. He wondered why history had given all the credit to some English lieutenant named Maynard. Feeling the glory of this most extraordinary moment, he looked down at the glowering intent that still emanated from Blackbeard's death mask.

"Cap'n, 'istory was wrong!" Knox said. "It's a fact that *we're* the ones what sent Blackbeard down to the old place."

The Phantom answered with his eyes.

Knox stood over Blackbeard where he had fallen. "Let's give this one the toss together, Cap'n."

Knox was right. It was only fitting that they be the ones, for this was a warrior's trophy, and theirs to claim. Understanding at once, Rosario smiled warmly. With Knox at the feet and Rosario at the shoulders, the two proceeded to pick up the still warm body. Rolling Blackbeard over onto his back was the easiest way for the two to hoist and heave. They lifted the corpse together and had it up between knee and waist high when the head separated at its laceration and fell back on the deck in a half roll, stopping at Mandoon's feet. The raw, hideous image escaped Knox and Rosario long enough for them to toss the headless corpse overboard before taking in what the frantic Maraudian had since turned away from. While the moment served to tie another knot in Mandoon's stomach, the same instant charged the boatswain with pride.

Knox was animated as he scooped up the head by the top hair. "It's the legend, Cap'n!"

Rosario smiled. "You mean the head business?"

"Aye, Cap'n, we're the ones alright! The 'ead, Cap'n, the 'ead and all the rest!"

Rosario glared at his boatswain. "All that other business?"

Mandoon had reached his limit. "I'm ready to go, Captain," he called out. "I can do it now!"

Knowing Mandoon's delicate state, the Phantom answered the panic-stricken wizard, who was already standing in the position necessary for successful reentry.

"Very well, Mandoon," he said. "Prepare to get under way in one quarter hour."

"Very well, Captain," was Mandoon's response. Grimacing, he closed his eyes and waited.

Turning to Knox, Rosario snapped the order, "We must get the crew into position before he takes us back!"

"Aye, Cap'n!" Knox was on it even though he was still holding Blackbeard's head by its bloodied black curls. The valiant boatswain barked orders to his brother seamen to prepare for the return trip. "On deck!" he hollered. "We're goin' back now while we still can. Remember, mates, you must be in your exact positions…, the same as when we left."

Preoccupied by something on the port side, most of the crew failed to hear Knox's orders. As if to accent the moment, double plumes of cannon shot fell into the sea, nearly hitting the sloop as it tried to beg off.

Rosario saw two sloops approaching, newcomers, flying British colors. He could make out the lead ship, the *Ranger*, a British pirate hunter, no doubt, which would be here soon.

"Quickly!" Mandoon shrieked. "Get into position, eyes front! We're leaving!"

"Let's get out of here *now*!" Rosario called.

"Belay that, Cap'n!" Knox countermanded, as more and more of the crew became aware of what was happening on the port side, where the *Queen Anne's Revenge* had yet to get under way.

Mandoon froze when he saw what they were all looking at. There, in blood-drenched aqua blue waters, amidst floating corpses and drowning wounded pirates, was the most ghastly and unnerving spectacle of this day.

"My God, Cap'n!" Knox howled. "'Ow can it be?" He could not believe his eyes.

Rosario stood transfixed with his crew at the hideous sight in the water that defied reason. Blackbeard's headless body was swimming effortlessly around its own ship, evoking cries of horror from the survivors on the *Queen Anne's Revenge*.

Knox stood mesmerized with the severed head still in hand. After twenty years at sea, he thought he had seen everything, but this was more than a bloody battle. This day had delivered them to the very gates of hell.

"Get rid of it!" Rosario commanded, white with terror.

Coming out of his trance, Knox flung the gory trophy toward the royal sloop. Blackbeard's severed head splashed into the bloodstained water. Then it surfaced with its eyes bulging and bobbed about among the other carnage.

A second barrage came in from the British sloops, narrowly missing the *Jewel* and the headless swimmer.

"Cap'n," Knox cried, "they're shooting at everybody!"

"All hands, take your positions *now*!" Rosario yelled, giving Mandoon a nod. "We're leaving! To your positions! We're out of time!"

III

It turned out that very few of the crew were in their correct positions. Even Rosario could not resist taking one last look before everything vanished. After the flash of white light, they were back. Now only the heavily damaged *Jewel* drifted where just a moment before there was so much flotsam of death and destruction.

"We have returned," Mandoon confirmed as he stepped away from the time portal.

By the sun's position, it was four hours past sunrise. Conditions were perfect—warm, calm, and clear. At any other time, the lack of appreciable wind would not have been so welcome. In her present tenuous condition, punctured like Swiss cheese and rudderless, the haggard *Jewel* could not have handled anything more rigorous.

Ironically, Mandoon still had his wits about him when they arrived back at their point of origin. Besides Mandoon, of the one hundred and fifty crew members who had survived the sea battles, only thirty men had made it back to the present alive, twenty-six of them with no harm whatsoever. Of the other four, three were incoherent with vacant expressions. The fourth was Rosario, who had been standing next to Knox during the time travel. The boatswain had remained unscathed, but the captain had been unable to resist one last look at Blackbeard's body swimming without its head. In that half-second in which he lingered before returning to the correct alignment, his mind's eye perceived the essence of the day's horror, leaving his facial expression permanently transfixed in a hidious wide-eyed glare. He had been branded by the images of the horrific chain of events that had him in tow. The rest of the crew never made it back to their positions and lay dead where they had stood.

When Knox looked at the captain, he immediately noticed that the expression on his face was one he had never seen on the Phantom before. His bushy eyebrows were almost pushed off by the rippled wrinkles across his forehead. His gaze, always penetrating, now took on an abnormal wide-eyed intensity.

After one look at what had happened, Mandoon wasted no time in activating the homing beacon intended for the treasure ship. He would take his chances with Terran. Whatever he might suffer under his own captain was far preferable to spending any more time with these poor swabs.

"Where is the *Tortuga Diablo*?" asked Rosario, seeming to come around as he looked out to sea in all directions.

"There's no one to be seen, Cap'n," Knox replied, looking over to where Mandoon was sitting beside the time portal.

The science officer was holding something that flashed a small pulsating red beam.

"Mandoon!" Knox hollered, startling him. "'Ave we arrived in the right place?"

"There's no room for error," replied the space wizard. "Returning back to the same spot is an absolute certainty."

"It's true," said Rosario, "we were delayed a few days by Mandoon's fear of returning to face his captain, but that doesn't explain why Pizzo and the ship aren't here waiting for us."

"Aye, Cap'n," Knox agreed. "They would 'ave waited weeks, if need be. It don't make sense. What could 'ave 'appened to 'em?"

"Just what we need...," said Rosario, scowling, "another mystery!"

"Aye, Cap'n," said Knox. "But we'd better be gettin' to matters at 'and. We're in a pityful state..., driftin', listin', and rudderless."

"Right you are, Mr. Knox," said Rosario. "To matters at hand, then!"

By midday, the twenty-six healthy crew members were moving about the ship, burying the dead and assessing the damage. The ship's head carpenter, Joaquin, started work on the destroyed rudder, estimating that he would have it operational within a day. Once the rudder was repaired, they would be able to get under way. Reefing the sails had paid off. Protected in this way, they had remained intact, ready to take the *Jewel* back to port.

Mandoon's homing beacon had been operational for several

hours before Rosario discovered it. "Damn and blast!" he said. "That bilge rat Terran is the last one I want to see. Their kind won't be satisfied until they've killed us all."

Knox had not yet adjusted to Rosario's ghastly, penetrating glare. It made his words sound more like a prophecy of doom than an assessment of the enemy's intent.

"I agree, Cap'n," he said, "but I don't know 'ow we can avoid 'em. If that device of Mandoon's is worth its salt, we'll be seein' their sky barge before long."

Looking skyward, the Phantom shuddered.

"We've got to get away somehow," he said. "One thing is certain. I'll not be going on any more of their missions."

His determination to escape Terran's clutches had not wavered. Rosario was disturbed. That much was evident to anyone who knew him and looked into his deranged visage. But he still had his wits about him.

Normally, the absence of wind was a matter of concern to any sailor, but at this moment, it was the answer to an unspoken prayer. The lack of breeze brought a healing calm to the stricken *Jewel*. She was in need of extensive refitting, but for now she would have to get home as best she could. Smashed woodwork and torn rigging covered what was left of her battered weather deck. While the two main masts were still intact, the aft mast was greatly weakened and had lost all of the fine Indian cotton sails that gave the great ship her edge. The hull was still tight and seaworthy. Once the rudder was refitted, sailing her back to Turtle Island would be slow but steady.

"Everything we have left," said Rosario to Knox, "is aboard the *Blue Dolphin*, and by all that's holy, that space dog won't find where we sunk her. We must find the *Tortuga Diablo*. She's our only hope now!"

Hearing the familiar passion and resolve in the Phantom's voice, Knox was able to overlook his captain's grotesque face. He had been with Rosario from the beginning and would follow him anywhere.

"We'll find 'er, Cap'n. We'll find 'er," he said, meeting his captain's stare with a warm smile.

Approaching from behind the two men, Mandoon overheard their whole conversation about the sunken treasure. When he discovered their secret, he withdrew back to where he had been sitting by the time portal. The crafty wizard's mind raced with the possibilities while he waited for Terran, uncertain whether the *Maraudor* was still in range of his signal.

They're planning to run north, hoping Terran will lose interest. Not likely, unless he's already left, thinking we've been lost. If he gets this signal, he won't leave until he has all of Rosario's treasure.

What Mandoon did not know was that Knox had seen him spying on him and the captain.

"We'll have to assume he heard everything," said Rosario, "which means he knows about the treasure on the *Blue Dolphin*. We'll have to eliminate him."

Mandoon's theory of correct positioning and focus is what saved the few crew members who managed to follow the space wizard's instructions during the melee with Blackbeard. Another side effect that Mandoon had failed to consider was the time displacement that occurred with these temporal jaunts.

To those who were waiting for the return of the time travelers, six weeks had elapsed since the *Jewel* left on its escapade. Since the mission was expected to have taken seventy-two hours at most, after two weeks of waiting, both the Maraudians and the crew of the *Tortuga Diablo* had given up hope of the *Jewel* ever returning. With the loss of the time portal on the *Jewel*, Terran focused his operations in the China Sea, barely keeping an eye on the *Tortuga Diablo*.

Terran was euphoric when he started receiving Mandoon's signal, and set an immediate course for its point of origin. He was elated because now he could fulfill his latest obsession. While doing business in the China Sea, he had discovered the fifteenth-century story and records of the Grand Eunuch Cheng Lo and his prodigious expeditions, which involved thirty thousand men and three hundred ships—sixty-two of which were filled with treasure. According to the records, the treasure ships were as long as four hundred and fifty-three feet.

Every written word about the illustrious Grand Eunuch served to increase the frenzy of greed that erupted within the terrible Terran. The opulence of these expeditions, in fact, was overwhelming for any Maraudian. Treasure of this magnitude pushed them into the state of obsession known as the Rapture.

Once Terran learned about this incredible fortune, he could not stop thinking about it. At first, he had hoped against hope that the Jewel would return with the portal. He knew that, given the chance, he would not hesitate to use the device again, regardless of the risk.

There were many records, reports, and notated maps dating back to the epic expeditions of the Grand Eunuch, even inventory lists of all sixty-two treasure ships.

If I only had the time portal! With this information, I could pull off the greatest single haul in the three known galaxies.

He figured things out, front and back.

Without any help from the Earthmen, I could take my own ship back to 1405 and stun the lot of them in a single afternoon.

Terran knew all the details by heart, having pored over them during the sleepless nights that followed the loss of his science officer, time portal, and all his human guinea pigs.

But now, with the appearance of Mandoon's signal, he felt more than a glimmer of hope.

In times like these, Commander Zalcon had a better grip on appropriate priorities than Terran did. Seeking to temper his captain's exuberance with the obvious pressing obstacles, he said, "Of course, Captain, it still remains to be seen if they have returned in acceptable condition…if, indeed, they have returned at all."

Terran only heard his own choir in the first mate's words. "*If?* Why, of *course* it's them! Who else could it be?"

"Even so, Captain, something must have happened to them. Where have they been all this time? These are answers we must have before we risk ourselves on such a journey."

The preoccupied captain nodded in tacit agreement.

The look of unbridled excitement in the captain's eyes made Zalcon uneasy.

Homing in on Mandoon's signal, the space barge was soon hovering over the wounded *Jewel* just as Rosario and Knox were only moments away from slitting Mandoon's throat.

"Blasted scum suckers!" cursed Rosario, "Now we've had it for sure. We have to keep playing along with Terran. It's the only way out, if indeed one exists at all."

"Right, Cap'n," said Knox, "we'll do our bit."

As soon as Terran, Zalcon, and three other Maraudians came aboard, they headed toward Rosario on the quarterdeck. Mandoon met them amidships, talking frantically.

"I'm sure 'e's tellin' 'em all about the Blue Dolphin, Cap'n," said Knox. "Aye, and by the looks of it, 'e's blamin' us for the 'ole bloody mess."

"Enough!" Terran shouted at Mandoon as he held up his hand. "All I want to know is if the time portal is still operational!"

"Oh yes, Captain," Mandoon said, pointing to it. "And we have solved the problem of cerebral abrasion. Even though only thirty of them survived this mission, the others perished because they were not in their correct positions for reentry."

It was obvious to Terran and Zalcon that Mandoon had been

shaken by his ordeal. Whether he was telling them everything that had happened was of little concern to them at this point. All that really mattered was that they had the time portal back in their possession and that the science officer had solved the problem of reentry in the time-traveling process.

Cringing in anticipation of his captain's wrath over the failed mission, Mandoon was taken by surprise when Terran said in a low voice, "Losing the prize was not your fault. You did your job. And this *Blue Dolphin* intelligence is also compensation. You have safely navigated back, even though you are late. You have solved our problems, and now we can use the tool ourselves."

Terran's expression did not in any way resemble a smile, but there was a warmth in his choice of words that calmed the nervous wizard.

Actually, Terran was pleased with the miscalculating Mandoon. The fact that Rosario and his men had been maimed and ruined in the process meant nothing to him. Terran was exhilarated knowing that his new plan for plundering Cheng Lo's dynasty was now doable.

Once again, Mandoon cringed as his captain looked around, this time noticing that the aft sonic cannon had been demolished.

But with a sweeping gesture toward the forward cannon, Terran said, "And we still have one weapon intact, I see." With this, he turned to his first officer and ordered, "Have the men prepare the gun to be removed!"

"At once, Captain," said Zalcon.

To Mandoon's great relief, nothing more was said about the lost sonic cannon.

As Rosario and Knox stood on the quarterdeck, watching the space pirates approach, their blood began to boil. The urge to slaughter Terran and his whole lot, right there on the spot, could barely be suppressed within the Earthlings.

Maybe this is our last chance, thought Rosario, *the only chance we'll ever get.*

But realizing there was no future in it, he decided to bide his time and keep his desperate thoughts to himself.

While Zalcon carried out Terran's orders, the Maraudian captain came up to Rosario. As they stood three feet apart, their eyes locked. The Phantom's maniacal wide-eyed expression was unsettling, but Terran pretended not to notice.

Countering the torment raging behind Rosario's eyes, Terran said, "It is good to see you made it back, Captain. It looks like you have been through a lot, and all for naught. At least, you still have the *Tortuga Diablo* and a crew...and not a small amount of treasure from our other missions."

Rosario ignored the bait that Terran was chumming with. His new wide-eyed intensity bore into Terran as the Maraudian braced his façade against the Phantom's intimidating gaze.

As wily as ever, Rosario still knew his priorities. "Where *is* the *Tortuga Diablo*?" he demanded.

"In Tortuga, of course," Terran replied smugly. "She has not moved out of the bay in the last four of the six weeks you've been missing."

"Six *weeks*, you say?!" Rosario gasped in disbelief.

Knox's eyebrows almost touched his hairline when he heard this. "*That's* why no one was waitin' when we got back, Cap'n," he said.

Continuing to keep some semblance of the partnership alive, the space pirate patronized Rosario. "Are you going to be able to navigate back to Tortuga, Captain?"

In his reassuring manner, the cosmic con man was seeking to discover where Rosario had hidden all the treasure he knew he still had. If Terran could get a clue where to look for that, he could soon leave for his time mission in the China Seas.

The Phantom's mind was ablaze with the urge to take Terran out, regardless of the consequences. But Rosario remained stone-faced as Knox answered for him: "To be sure, Cap'n. We'll be under way by late tomorrow or the next day for sure."

"We will be a while dismantling the cannon," Terran said. "Is there anything we can help you with in your preparations?"

The Maraudian was pleased to carry on the conversation with Knox, tactfully ignoring Rosario's detachment.

But Knox fell silent now, ignoring this empty gesture.

"No, thank you, Captain Terran," said Rosario, coming back into the moment. "I think you have done quite enough!"

The Phantom's strained response was followed by an agonizing moment of silence that caused Knox to grimace.

Always at his best, Terran simply let Rosario's words settle unchallenged. Wasting no more time with pleasantries, he ordered, "Zalcon, hoist the time portal!"

Rosario and Knox watched the Maraudians from the quarterdeck as they gathered around the device and lifted it into the hemp basket.

"Take it and good riddance, I say," Knox muttered, voicing what the rest of the crew members were thinking.

Rosario added, "But it's never that simple with these greedy blackguards. They won't leave till they've taken all we have left."

Terrible as they were true, these words made Knox shudder.

With all of their gear offloaded, the Maraudians departed.

Zalcon waved, calling, "We'll be back soon."

Watching the hemp basket ascend to the space barge, Rosario continued, "As long as they don't know where our stash is hidden, they still need us. Once they find out, they'll have no further use for us. We've got to get to Tortuga and the ship. We'll make a run for the Great Northern Wilds carrying only supplies and gunpowder. Maybe they'll decide to cut their losses and give up on us, and all the while, we won't be near any treasure. They can't stand *that* for very long. All that matters now is to get away from them before they send us under."

"Aye, Cap'n, to be sure," Knox said consolingly. He knew Rosario better than the captain knew himself. Although the plan to escape to the north was basically sound, the truth was that the idea of leaving any treasure behind would prove to be unacceptable to the battered and beaten Phantom.

By mid-morning, Joaquin had the rudder repaired and operational.

Rosario started for Tortuga with the lumbering *Jewel*. Averaging six knots, they would arrive in less than two days.

Terran would have left the haggard crew of the Phantom forever, had it not been for that bit of treasure he knew they were hiding. But for now, all he could do was to start planning the Cheng Lo mission, the most important one yet.

Convinced that any objections to further use of the time portal would be futile, Zalcon joined his captain in prioritizing the next jaunt through time.

The first thing the commander suggested when they were onboard the sky barge was that they put the Hat on Mandoon. "It's the only way to find out what really happened," he said. Zalcon reveled in the smirk of approval that came over his captain's imperious features as Terran took a moment to bask in his first officer's competence.

"Agreed," said Terran. "We'll put the Hat on him first thing after we all get some rest."

Terran already had the tactical side of his plan worked out. All that remained was to confirm Mandoon's findings on the technical fine points of safe time travel. "No matter what," he said, "we must secure the last of Rosario's stash when we return from this mission. We won't leave the planet without it!"

Zalcon understood his captain's zeal when it came to treasure. "Yes, Captain. Sleep well, sir."

The two men each retired to their quarters.

As Zalcon drifted off to sleep, he wondered: *If, by some miracle, Terran's plan to loot sixty-two treasure ships is successful, will he still come back for Rosario's pitiful remnant of a treasure trove? He probably would…. I would.*

While Terran was busy dreaming about the Far East, the *Tortuga Diablo* lay in Turtle Bay. Captain Pizzo had assumed permanent command of what was left of the Phantom's crew, and had taken Aleia for his own. Like Rosario, he was reluctant to have any further dealings with the Maraudians. He also had no intention of leaving behind what was left of their plunder. Day after day, he sat in the bay, afraid to make a move to recover the sunken treasure until he was certain the space pirates were gone.

Able-bodied seaman James Villa had been a member of the Phantom's crew since the beginning, and was still adjusting to the fact that Rosario and all his mates were never coming back. There were barely enough men left now to sail the *Tortuga Diablo*, not that they were apt to go anywhere so long as the space pirates were still hanging around. Villa and the rest of the crew had agreed with Captain Pizzo when he told Terran that until Rosario and the *Jewel* returned, all operations would cease. For the past four weeks, they had kept a low profile while meticulously preparing the ship to leave the bay at a moment's notice.

As Captain Pizzo waited for the chance to get away from the Maraudians, it was beginning to look like his plan was working.

It had been a month since their last contact with Terran.

The sweltering afternoon sun still had a few hours before it would sear the aquamarine sapphire with its crimson surrender. Villa was overseeing the re-rigging of a new Indian-spun topsail. High above the weather deck, he had a commanding view of the infamous Tortuga Bay, which had hosted dozens of sloops, brigs, and galleons in the golden age of buccaneers just one hundred years before. Now only the *Tortuga Diablo* lay anchored in the bay on the leeside of Turtle Island. The waning age of the buccaneer weighed heavily on Villa's heart, along with everything else that seemed to be stifling the only life he knew.

In the midst of these thoughts, he looked out on the horizon and saw a set of sails pop out from the tip of the island. Watching the craft until it became a full silhouette against the golden sunshine, Villa could not believe his eyes, even though he could recognize the ship anywhere. His mates, unaware of the sighting, continued their work atop the main mast. In another moment, Villa was sure beyond a doubt.

"Sails ho! *Caramba!* It's the *Jewel!* It's the *Jewel*, I tell ya!"

Two of his three mates almost lost their grip when Villa's alarm startled them from their work.

Word traveled fast across the weather deck and to the captain's quarters.

Pizzo's heart went to his throat as he sprang to his feet, exclaiming, "Could this be true?"

"So, what if it is?" Aleia demanded. "I'm *your* woman now."

Pizzo clearly knew that he was not going to choose the

woman over his loyalty to Rosario or their brotherhood.

If he's not dead, the grand cabin belongs to him..., and so does she!

Pizzo turned to face the enchantress, whose powers suddenly seemed diminished.

"You are the captain's woman," he said sternly. "When Rosario returns, I will no longer be captain. You must return to him and make the best of it."

Pizzo's heart ached with the anticipation of no longer basking in the adoration of the sea goddess, but for him there could be no other choice. He would not sacrifice his code of honor and his allegiance. His life as Rosario's fleet captain and their brotherhood were paramount, beyond any doubt or reconsideration.

"If you know what's good for you, Aleia," he warned, "you'll play along with him. One thing's for sure...you don't want to make him rage. If you're not careful, your life will become unbearable. In a few days, we can explain that we thought he was dead, and as long as he has his way, we'll all have a big laugh over how it all worked out, to be sure. Otherwise, you'll witness a side of the man seldom seen and never survived."

As Pizzo left the cabin, the finality of his words lingered while the gypsy queen quickly calculated her position in this new reality. Usually, she would have arrived at the obvious priority, put aside her own preferences, and gone back to pampering Rosario. It was the first time that this part of her process seemed impassable. Love had an uncompromising hold on her, and hard as she might try, she knew that some other way would have to be found.

Captain Pizzo joined most of the crew on the bow, where he immediately recognized the *Jewel* as she came around the island's lee. They would be dropping anchor in another hour.

Their coded signals kept repeating the same five messages:

WE ARE BACK
MISSION FAILED
TWENTY-SEVEN SURVIVORS
TERRAN WANTS BLUE DOLPHIN
MAKE READY TO SAIL

After repeating these signals several times, the flagman on the Jewel paused, waiting for a response.

Pizzo signaled back:

UNDERSTOOD

"She looks a bit the worse for the wear, Cap'n," said Ben Wilkes, who had been looking through Pizzo's telescope and now handed it back to him.

After a few minutes' observation, it was obvious to Pizzo that the *Jewel* had taken a pummeling.

I wonder who's still alive of all those mates?

They would not have long to wait for answers to the myriad questions forming onboard the *Tortuga Diablo*.

It suddenly occurred to Pizzo that there was a chance Rosario might not be among the ones returning. He grimaced at the possibility that he had spoken prematurely to Aleia.

Steadily, the *Jewel* came into the bay and dropped her anchor fifty yards off the port bow of the *Tortuga Diablo*. Recognizing the familiar profile bringing the ship to anchorage, Pizzo had the answer to his question. Rosario was still alive and in command. Relieved that he had made the right move with the woman, he watched as Rosario, Knox, and Joaquin were the first of the survivors to start for the *Tortuga Diablo*.

In the time that remained before they came aboard, Pizzo told the brotherhood that Rosario would be the boss the moment he stepped onto the deck. "Everything will be back under his command, just as it was. This, of course, includes the woman. She's the captain's woman. We thought he was dead. Well, we were mistaken, and so we must adjust accordingly. I tell you these things to clear the air and so you can realize that this is how it is, now that the Phantom has returned."

Pizzo's final speech as captain of the *Tortuga Diablo* was well received. In fact, the crew seemed a bit relieved. Only Aleia remained torn and dismal as she stayed in her quarters, trying to come to grips with losing Pizzo and having to return to Rosario, all in a matter of a few hours. In the end, she would rely on her practical side. She had a name for these unbearable transitions that occurred from time to time in the life she had chosen.

"It's a stormy day," she would say. Then, taking a deep breath, she would face whatever she was compelled to deal with. When Rosario climbed aboard, she knew she would do what she must to get through *this* stormy day.

In another hour, the orange giant would sink beneath the vermilion horizon. As Rosario's men pulled for the *Tortuga Diablo*, the Phantom sat back in the longboat, gazing at his flagship, which was resting easy and unscathed in the golden amber light. Only the need to escape Terran was powerful enough to share space in his mind with his ever-present thoughts of Aleia.

Rosario felt some relief as he stepped from launch to ladder. The crew on the *Tortuga Diablo* cheered as he came aboard, but they could see immediately that things were not right with their captain.

Pizzo was first to greet the boarding party: "Welcome aboard and welcome back, Captain!"

The words were only half out of his mouth when he noticed the startling and hideous expression on the Phantom's face. The two men stood staring at each other, Rosario still reeling from his ordeal, and Pizzo momentarily stunned as he tried to come to grips with what he was seeing.

Knox broke the spell. "Cap'n Pizzo," he said heartily, "it's good to be back. As you can see, we've been through a lot and barely escaped with our lives. There are only twenty-seven of us left. Everyone else was lost."

Now Rosario took command. "We've got to get the *Tortuga Diablo* ready," he said. "We must escape the pirate devils. They mean to take what little treasure we have left before they send us all down to the old place."

"I agree, Captain," Pizzo replied. "In fact, we're almost ready now. We've been preparing for just such a plan. But, Captain, do you realize you've been gone almost seven weeks?"

Rosario nodded.

"We thought you were all lost, Captain. But now let's get the rest of the crew aboard, and then we can decide when and where to make our move."

"Where's Aleia?" Rosario demanded.

"You'll find her in your quarters, sir."

Nodding, the Phantom said, "We should get under way as soon as possible. I'll show you the plan in the morning. Send food to my quarters." Not waiting for a response, he started toward the grand cabin.

"Aye, Captain," Pizzo called.

She heard his boots hit the quarterdeck as they took the dozen steps to the grand cabin. Wiping her eyes dry and blowing her nose softly into her hanky, she was as ready as she would ever be.

The door flew open, with Rosario's figure blocking the light. His eyes had her riveted.

"Aleia, I'm back!"

She was in command of the shock and horror she felt, as her irrepressible survival instinct guided her through the effect of Rosario's hideous expression. His voice sounded sincere, which also helped her to keep from showing her revulsion. As he started toward her, she backed up against the bulkhead.

"What happened?" she countered. "Where were you?"

Her questions were only a device to keep some distance from the wide-eyed and haggard man.

Stopping when her hand met his chest, he answered, "I've

been through too much to tell you. I've lost most of my crew. All that matters now is that I have you back again. Are you *not* happy to see me?"

He took a step back, waiting for her answer.

"I thought you were lost, never to return. You must understand…, I'm confused. I need time to adjust to what's happening. You look terrible. You must need food, rest, and a bath."

He was relieved, realizing that he must look a frightful mess.

"Yes, of course, you're right," he said. "Draw me a bath."

His words had sufficient warmth to cut through the effect of his unnerving glare.

"At once, my captain," she said, and went out to the quarterdeck to tell Zabor, the cabin boy, to fetch water for the captain's bath.

When she returned to the cabin, Rosario was undressing. As she looked at him, she could not imagine enduring this night with him. She was used to going from one captain to the next, but in the past it had always been of her own choosing. She found it intolerable to be compelled to do so.

Suddenly, there was a knock at the door. It was a crew member with the captain's supper.

Rosario poured water into a brass bowl to wash his hands and face. Bending over the bowl, he saw for the first time his warped wide-eyed expression.

What have those blackguards done to me? Now I understand why she drew back. What am I to do? I'm doomed.

As Rosario stood with his back to the woman, Aleia took from her collection of potions a greenish powder, with which she gave his meal a light dusting.

He was more hungry than amorous at the moment, so she had little trouble getting him to the table. Nevertheless, she placated him with promises of how they would spend the rest of the evening.

During the meal, Zabor prepared his captain's bath. Afterward, while Aleia was washing Rosario's back, the Phantom tried to tell her why they must be away from here before another day passed.

His words meant less to her than the sound of the light chop that was slapping the hull. She understood very little of what he said about the Maraudians. Lost in her own thoughts, she wondered how she would ever get back to Pizzo.

After his bath, Rosario staggered over to the bed. Trying not to be obvious, Aleia lit the cabin lights, pretending to be almost ready to lie with him. Delaying as long as possible, she finally came to the bed. To her great relief, her potion had worked: Rosario was fast asleep and would remain so until the sun was high in the sky.

At daybreak, the weather deck was bustling as the crew finished refitting the ship with new sails and stocking the provisions they would need. Trading with the local population for oxen and pig was easy, and the reason why the Phantom's fleet anchored here whenever possible.

By late morning, Rosario was awake with a thousand

thoughts running through his mind like a school of flying fish. But by the time he arrived on the quarterdeck, he was focused only on his two foremost priorities.

Gazing at his captain's face, Pizzo braced himself. "Good morning, sir," he said.

Acknowledging Pizzo's greeting with a nod, the Phantom looked around. "It's late. Where's Aleia?"

"I haven't seen her yet this morning," Pizzo replied.

The truth was that Aleia had been in Pizzo's quarters at six bells, pleading with him to take her back. To this he had flatly refused, demanding that she return at once to the grand cabin.

Rosario sucked in a deep breath of the revitalizing sea air, holding it as long as he could before exhaling long and slowly.

"Never mind," he said. "We've got to make ready to sail. Can we be under way before tomorrow?"

"Aye, Captain," Pizzo responded. "We can leave on the midnight tide."

Satisfied with Pizzo's answer to his second question, Rosario took another deep breath of sea air and said, "We need to get as far away as we can from these blackguards as soon as possible. We'll head for the Great Northern Wilds."

The crew spent the rest of that day preparing for departure. Pizzo and the captain made a complete inspection of the ship and ship's stores before consulting sea charts and planning their escape to the north. But there was one piece of business that Pizzo had been avoiding all day. Now it was the only issue that remained.

"Captain," he said, "we still have a considerable amount of treasure aboard."

Rosario's wide-eyed expression became even more pronounced at the mention of the last remnants of his lost treasure trove.

"We'll take it with us!" he said, scowling.

Pizzo's mouth dropped. "But, Captain," he gasped, "that's what Terran's after. It will only make him more intent in his pursuit."

Rosario snapped back in scornful resentment, "I'll not surrender another piece of eight to that scoundrel!"

Pizzo said no more as the Phantom stalked off the bridge.

When Rosario entered the grand cabin, he found Aleia combing her hair.

Back on the *Maraudor*, Mandoon readily consented to meet Terran and Zalcon for the mind scan. They all hoped it would reveal any secrets remaining for the safe operation of the time portal. By the end of the first two-hour scanning session, they had only just begun to unravel the minute-by-minute story of the failed mission.

An invaluable aid to solving otherwise unknowable questions, the mind scanner—or the Hat, as it was sometimes called—still required a lot of their time and energy to sift through the data for nuggets of revelation. It would be over an hour before they could resume the scan.

Zalcon had many questions: *What took the mission six weeks,
and what exactly killed all those sailors? More importantly, how
do we prevent it from happening again?*

To uncover and analyze the details of Mandoon's experiences would take at least a dozen sessions with the Hat. They
would have to proceed slowly, so as not to exhaust the science
officer's mental faculties. Taking advantage of the rest time to
evaluate the latest data, they slowly began to piece together what
had happened to cause the obvious time discrepancy.

The third scanning session answered that question. There
was a trapezoidal effect when traveling through time, a fact that
they discovered as the scan proceeded. Mandoon had forgotten
this aspect of temporal theory, which stated that as you travel
back in time or toward the center, the temporal sphere continues
to get smaller. From this, they were able to calculate that if going
back a hundred years lost six weeks, then Terran's proposed mission back to the fifteenth century would cost them the equivalent
of at least twenty weeks of the present time.

As Terran discussed these things with Zalcon, the captain
realized that they would have to get Rosario's hidden stash
before leaving for the ancient Chinese Empire. He decided that
as soon as the scanning sessions were finished, they would pay
Rosario a visit and give *him* a turn or two with the Hat.

Mandoon submitted humbly to each scan, as many as four a
day. Knowing that Terran and Zalcon would see the real chain
of events, he consoled himself with the thought that he was back

among his own kind, a condition he found infinitely preferable to what he had just been through.

After a dozen sessions, Terran had the answers to most of his questions and was feeling optimistic about his next adventure. The first mission had failed to secure any treasure. But it was a small price to pay for the knowledge gained about the safe operation of the time portal.

Nearly a week had passed since the Maraudians' last contact with Rosario. But when they arrived back over Tortuga Bay, the Phantom's flagship was nowhere to be seen. Only the battered *Jewel* lay anchored and deserted where the *Tortuga Diablo* had been.

Since Rosario's midnight escape from Tortuga Bay, the brig of war, running with a broad beam reach, was averaging over two hundred miles per day. They had left the fair weather behind. It was not hurricane season, but the sky was threatening. Onboard, the mood was tentative. Running north was never good for morale; running from a predator in the sky was not only unnerving, it was surreal.

Rosario was beginning to realize that things were different between himself and the enchantress. Using one excuse after another, she had managed to avoid him for most of each day, but she could not keep this up much longer. Each evening she had skillfully tricked the Phantom into a dreamless sleep, thus avoiding the intimacies she would allude to during the day.

When Rosario realized she was drugging him every night, he became enraged.

"You wicked strumpet! You and your potions! Did you really think I wouldn't notice?"

To his surprise, she denied nothing. "It's true," she said. "Things have changed between us. I'm in love with Pizzo... even though he won't have me."

Rosario reeled from his sudden loss. Then, as his broken heart turned his thoughts toward revenge, his dark side emerged.

A maniacal expression came over his contorted face as he stormed out of the grand cabin. Seeking solace on the fantail, he stood planted on the rolling deck, holding on to the taffrail with both hands, glaring out to sea, trying to come to grips with yet another devastating loss.

In spite of his crumbled heart, his rage for Terran still burned white hot within. Terran was the cause of all that was destroying him. Now he had lost the most important treasure of all. Rosario was no longer able to contain his rage, as his feeling for Terran and Aleia's betrayal merged into one overpowering fury, which swept him over the edge into the madness that Pizzo had warned Aleia of.

The wind was steadily increasing all afternoon, reaching gale force as the night ensued. While all hands rigged the ship for the oncoming storm, Rosario obsessed over a plan to do away with Aleia.

"If *I* can't have her, no one will," he muttered to himself as he sought out his own secret potion. Two drops of the clear oil would be all that was needed to send her into an endless sleep.

Outside the grand cabin, the coming storm promised a

tumultuous sea as it continued to rock the vessel. Inside, Aleia sat wringing her hands, unsure of what her next move should be. Suddenly, the door flew open as Rosario entered, carrying two mugs.

Despite his facial affliction and the rage that burned within his chest, he managed to convey a sheepish attitude as he offered her one of the mugs.

"I'm sorry for going off the way I did," he said. "I understand you thought I was dead and gone. I don't blame you for the way things are. I hope you can forgive my behavior."

Matching his pleasant tone, Aleia said, "It's true that no one was at fault. The way things turned out, we were both victims."

Rosario did not want to hear any consolation. He had made his move. Quickly finishing his drink, he excused himself and left for the bridge.

Minutes after drinking what she thought was hot buttered rum, Aleia knew she had been poisoned. Her mind raced with panic. Realizing that her fate was irreversible, embittered by the loss of her one true love, and convinced of Rosario's fiendish ways, she resolved to take Pizzo with her, thus sparing him a fate worse than death.

She sent Zabor to summon her lover to her side. In the midst of the growing gale, the first mate broke away from his duties on the quarterdeck to answer her call. Rosario pretended not to notice as Pizzo stole away.

When he arrived at the grand cabin, Aleia, like Rosario, also feigned forgiveness and understanding. She asked her lover to join her in a farewell toast before they said goodbye forever. Agreeing, he sat down at the long table, saying that it would be the best thing to do for the both of them. Raising their drinks, they toasted for the last time and emptied their goblets. Pizzo never knew what hit him as he sprawled out over the table.

The Phantom's potion was slower. Aleia was still alive, but failing steadily. She decided to end it now instead of waiting for Rosario's poison to dictate the moment of her death. Taking a pistol from its rack on the bulkhead, she sat on the bed and loaded it. Then, she turned the weapon on herself and pulled back the hammer.

At that moment, the door swung open and Rosario stepped in, wide-eyed and crazed. Almost in reflex, she aimed at him and fired. Rosario ducked. But Aleia would never know that her shot had missed its mark. With eyes still open, her head dropped over her breasts as the pistol fell out of her hand.

Now the storm unleashed its full fury, and the sea became a series of liquid mountains and valleys that tossed the *Tortuga Diablo* like a light canoe.

Rosario was thrown against the bulkhead and knocked unconscious as the storm took hold of the ship.

When they discovered the *Tortuga Diablo*'s disappearance, Terran and his party returned to the mother ship to consult their instruments. Because of the thick overcast that blanketed the whole Atlantic coast, finding the Phantom's whereabouts would be nearly impossible.

"Stay on it, we're not leaving until we find them," was all Terran had to say.

Annoyed but determined, the space pirates were not giving up as easily as the Phantom had hoped.

"Look at that!" Zalcon said. He was staring at a screen with Mandoon and three other technicians when they suddenly witnessed a phenomenon that they had only seen before in simulated training exercises. Just as Terran was joining them, the anomaly repeated itself. "There it is again!" Zalcon exclaimed. "Looks like a time spike! What else could it be?"

"Yes, a deliberate one!" Mandoon said. "See how it reoccurs seamlessly on the time map just *before* its predecessor?"

Turning to Mandoon and grasping his shoulder, Terran said, "I need more information."

The science officer responded immediately. "One of the many shoals in the sea of time travel," he explained, "is the contradiction that could arise from returning to your point of origin at a time prior to your departure. According to our current understanding, for a seamless round trip that will bring you back to the same reality that you left, you must return to the exact location, and at a time *after* the original time of departure. Returning *prior* to the original time of departure will place you in a new variation of your reality."

Mandoon's eloquence provided Terran with enough insight to grasp the meaning of what had just taken place. Only the stolen scanners of the Illuminosity were capable of reading and deciphering such phenomena. Although the Maraudians barely understood the equipment and could never repair it, without it they would not have had a clue as to what had just occurred.

"This would indicate," Mandoon said, "that the ones responsible for this time spike were trying to revise their reality by returning before their time of departure."

Nodding confidently, Terran concluded, "We'll have to go to where the time spikes occurred and see what's there. Mark the spot.... We'll go when the storm subsides."

As soon as Terran's words left his lips, Zalcon did a double take. "What's this?" he gasped, "The storm's over!"

As absurd as it sounded, the hurricane that had been raging in the area had vanished. In its place, a golden sun was making its late summer track across the cloudless blue vault of heaven.

"How can this be?" Terran demanded.

Mandoon was quick to reply. "They have created a new variation in reality,' he said. "There's only one way to find out what we're dealing with, Captain.... Let's get to the area in question."

"Agreed," said Terran. "Let's be on our way."

While Rosario recalled nothing of his dark adventures in the temporal limbo caused by the first time spike, the experience had left him with a new wisdom. The second time spike hurled him back to an earlier time when he was just beginning to doubt Aleia's affections. He decided to confide in Captain Pizzo, whose good counsel had always helped him around life's treacherous reefs.

Pizzo listened with baited breath as the captain shared his fears about the woman. When Pizzo began to bare *his* soul, he set the scene firmly in Rosario's mind.

"As you know, Captain, the woman is irresistible. We thought you and everyone on the *Jewel* were lost, never to return. We were left to carry on as best we could, and so the woman came to me because I had become the captain."

The Phantom remained silent all through Pizzo's enlightening confession. For a while, no one spoke.

Then Rosario said softly, "Yes, I understand. It's my loss..., another terrible wound from the last mission. You should go with her, my friend, if that's what you want. Things are different now, and she doesn't want me any longer. I can't be with a woman who doesn't want me. No one is to blame..., it's just the way things worked out."

Astonished, Pizzo listened in silence, relieved that there was no peace lost between them.

On the bridge of the *Maraudor*, Terran and his officers were visibly shaken when they discovered that the *Tortuga Diablo* and the Phantom were at the center of the time spike.

"Who is this Rosario?" Terran railed. "Phantom indeed! Activate the sonic cannons!"

"Whoever he is," Zalcon answered, "he has an advanced technique of time travel."

As their assessment of Rosario approached the absurd, they paused, perplexed.

"Perhaps he was incidental to the phenomenon," Mandoon offered. "It does not make sense that he would have such a command of this technology when he had to submit to ours."

Mandoon's theory allowed Terran and Zalcon to regain their sense of superiority.

"We'll get to the bottom of all this," said the captain. "It's time for Rosario's turn with the Hat. Prepare an armed boarding party."

"Yes, Captain, I'll see to it," Zalcon replied as he left the bridge.

It had been some march of days since Rosario had seen any signs of Terran, and it had been weeks for Pizzo and the others. A false sense of security was beginning to form on the *Tortuga Diablo* as another day unfolded without any trace of the space pirates.

"Things may be going back to the way they used to be, Captain," Pizzo said. "Maybe the Maraudians have left for good."

Rosario could only hope this was the case.

But it was not to be, for just at that moment, the sky barge reappeared hovering above the *Tortuga Diablo*.

Gazing upward to take in the golden haze of the sunset, Pizzo was jolted back to a harsh reality.

Instinctively he called out, "Sails ho!"

One look at Pizzo was all Rosario needed to know — the space pirates were back. A flush of despair swept over the Phantom. His heart sank with the terrible confirmation as the hemp basket began its descent.

"They could stun the lot of us if they wanted to," he muttered. "We've got no choice."

There was no more time to confer with Pizzo, for Terran, accompanied by Zalcon, Mandoon, and six armed crew members, was already coming aboard.

As Rosario and Pizzo approached, Terran said, "You two will be returning with us immediately to our ship for questioning."

The idea of being interrogated somewhere high above the Earth was absolutely unacceptable to Pizzo.

Bracing himself with one hand on his cutlass and the other on the rail, he declared, "Any questions you have, you can ask here and now!"

Without giving a thought to Pizzo's protest, Terran pointed at the defiant first mate, whereupon one of the armed guards drew his weapon and fired.

Pizzo collapsed from the sonic impact.

All of this unfolded in a matter of seconds.

Seeing her beloved fall, Aleia realized that her next opportunity was at hand. Although her scream started out from shock and loss, it ended in a pitch that had been honed by survival into frequencies that no male could resist.

The passionate tones of the siren stirred a lust within the

Maraudians that had been dormant since they had left their home planet. Although women were highly appreciated on Marauda, having a woman aboard was considered an absolute taboo, violation of which could bring only the worst consequences.

But smiling, Terran said, "No harm in looking."

Zalcon nodded as they turned, seeing Aleia for the first time.

Her beauty radiated like never before, instantly resurrecting their lust and threatening their judgment.

"Which one of you is the captain?" she asked.

Both men stared intensely, momentarily unable to respond.

Then Zalcon announced, "I am the first officer, and this is Captain Terran of the great ship *Maraudor*."

With these words, Zalcon ceased to exist for Aleia. She focused now entirely on the captain with the high energy of someone who enjoyed her work.

"I am yours now, Captain. I belong to you."

"You are certainly beautiful, Madame," Terran said coolly. "Perhaps the most beautiful woman I have ever seen. But I must decline your offer. You are not worth risking the wrath of Marauda."

Aleia was at a loss when she saw that her usual effect on men was not working. Until now, she had never met a man she could not conquer. Somehow, this one was different. Realizing that she had met her match, she withdrew to where Pizzo had fallen. Lifting his head onto her lap, she gently stroked his hair.

Zalcon and two of the armed detail came over to bring Pizzo

back for the interrogation.

"Not him," said Mandoon. "He's not the one you want. Take this one here...Knox, the boatswain. In my time with them, he was as close to their captain as any I've seen."

Without a word, Zalcon and his men turned and apprehended Knox where he was standing, close to the Phantom. Rosario was numb. He had seen too much already, and longed for it all to end. Now that the Maraudians' treacherous intentions were out in the open, his only hope was to somehow take Terran down with him. It was this thought alone that would sustain him through whatever came next.

As Knox followed Rosario into the hemp basket, the boatswain wondered if he would ever see the *Tortuga Diablo* again.

Terran and four of the armed guards took Rosario and Knox up to the sky barge, while Zalcon, Mandoon, and the other two guards waited aboard the *Tortuga Diablo* for the hemp basket to return.

"I wonder," said Mandoon, "how long it will take to get the answers to our questions from these Earthlings."

"For their sake," said Zalcon, "it had better not be long."

As Rosario and Knox waited on the sky barge for the retrieval of the rest of the landing party, they sat in a central compartment, which gave them a partial view of the mystifying circular chamber they were in. They could see four crew members attending the workstations and a band of video screens that spanned both sides of a much larger screen in the center. Above several columns of multicolored oscillating lights, each screen was lit with various colors and patterns that made no sense to the prisoners, but were entertaining to look at nonetheless. The larger screen in the center had a clear aerial view of the *Tortuga Diablo* below. This first look into Terran's world overwhelmed Rosario and Knox as they sat watching the marvelous controls and lights, and listening to the pulsating chirps and warbles of the craft.

When the second half of the landing party arrived onboard, the sky barge started back for the mother ship. During the ascent, Rosario and Knox were mesmerized as they watched the image of the *Tortuga Diablo* become smaller and smaller, until finally the big screen went blank.

Wasting no time, Terran decided to conduct his first interrogation during the return trip, hoping he could clear matters up even before he used the Hat.

"Did you create that time spike?" he asked. "And what happened to that hurricane?"

He asked these two questions over and over again, in as many different ways as he could. But neither of the prisoners had the slightest notion of what Terran was talking about.

The space pirate was confounded by the Earthlings' apparent ignorance—unless, of course, Mandoon was right, and they had been incidental to the phenomena.

This cursory first interrogation was interrupted as the sky barge connected to the mother ship with a gentle thud. Gone was the close feeling of the circular shuttlecraft as crew and prisoners passed through the hangar deck to a much larger chamber. As different as everything was for the buccaneers in this strange environment, the perpetual feeling of helplessness that started on the day that they had met the ruthless Maraudians remained as constant here as back in their own world.

The cold blue lighting of the oval corridor continued to hold Rosario and Knox transfixed as the captain escorted them past the glowing control panels and soft sounds toward their quarters. It was painfully obvious to them that things were profoundly different here in Terran's world.

On the way, Terran brought them past the bridge of his fantastic ship, where they were met with their first view from space. The panoramic scene was stunning. If it had been a bullet, it would have killed Rosario, but it was revelation, and he was reborn. His nineteenth-century depth perception melted away as he tried to make sense of what he was seeing.

"What am I looking at? Where are we?" he asked.

"We are looking at your world, the Earth and its moon, in the endless ocean of space," Terran said matter-of-factly.

He felt that this perspective would reinforce his captives' sense of inferiority while at the same time affording them an enlightening view that they would never have imagined. But he was concerned about their ability to cope with this look into the cosmos. He needed them to stay firm of mind so that they could undergo the series of scans he intended to conduct after they had slept.

The Earthlings would have been content to stand forever, gazing out into space. Terran indulged them a while longer, then dispatched them to quarters for rest.

Rosario and Knox had yet to utter a word since their first glimpse of their miniscule place in the Universe. Not until they were alone in their compartment did they speak.

"Cap'n," said Knox, "we're no match for these creatures."

His choice of words annoyed the Phantom. "If pirates be creatures," he said with a scowl, "then they be creatures indeed."

"Agreed, Cap'n. Let's give 'em what they want before they take it anyway."

"You're right. One thing's for sure, they won't have any need for us once they get what they want. We'll be lucky to get out of this alive."

"Aye, but it's our only chance of gettin' free from these devils, to be sure."

With that, the two drifted off into a restless sleep.

While the Phantom and Knox slept, the Maraudian officers conferred on how to proceed.

"It's the only thing that makes sense," Terran said, "so let's assume that you're right, Mandoon. They're not aware of what happened to them, or that there ever *was* a time spike."

"We must find out what we're dealing with," Mandoon replied.

"The only way to learn exactly what happened," said Zalcon, "is to proceed with the scans. That information is even more crucial than discovering the whereabouts of their treasure."

When Rosario and Knox awoke, they found cups of some kind of hot beverage on a table, along with two bowls of the Maraudian version of oatmeal. There was no way of telling how long they had slept. Their breakfast came just in time to keep the jagged edge of hunger from sinking them further into despair. Still weary from constant apprehension, but famished, they eagerly took their chances and gulped down the food and drink. Although unfamiliar, the taste was not unpleasant.

As they were finishing their meal, the hatch suddenly rolled back, and Mandoon stepped inside the compartment.

"We have questions and we need answers," said the spindly space wizard. "Captain Terran will meet with you soon on the science deck. I will—"

"There's no need for that," Rosario cut in. "We'll show you where the treasure is hidden in exchange for our freedom."

"Very well," Mandoon said, cackling. "But these are all things you should take up with the captain when you see him later." Pointing to Rosario, he went on, "*You* will be the first to meet with Captain Terran and Commander Zalcon. I shall return shortly to escort you to the science deck."

With that, he turned and left the compartment, with the hatchway immediately rolling shut behind him.

The buccaneers were not the type to give in easily, but after what they had seen since coming aboard the spaceship, they no longer had any vengeful ideas toward the Maraudians. Now, their only concern was to get away with their skins.

Knox hardly noticed Rosario's crazed expression anymore as they comforted each other with hopes of making it back home.

"The treasure's all they want," said Knox. "If we show 'em where it is and help 'em to get it, they won't have any reason to destroy us."

"Yes," said the captain, "escaping with our lives will be treasure enough."

Once again, the compartment door rolled open, and this time
Mandoon motioned Rosario to follow him.

Moving through the cold blue-lit passageways, the Phantom
felt a sense of awe about everything on Terran's incredible ship.
As he passed by different compartments, mostly manned, he
tried to form a mental picture of what the whole vessel might
look like.

Mandoon's station, the science section, was a tri-level set of
decks stacked with equipment. Terran and Zalcon were waiting
near the scanning equipment.

Rosario was ready for them and started in as soon as he
entered the room. "Captain Terran," he pleaded, "none of this is
necessary. I've decided to tell you everything…, if you will but
assure me that you will give Knox and myself safe passage back
to my ship."

"If the treasure is where you say it is," Terran agreed, "when
it is retrieved, you will have paid the price for your freedom."

Zalcon produced a chart of the Atlantic Ocean and spread it
out before Rosario, who immediately pointed to the exact location of the sunken *Blue Dolphin*.

"I'm sure, Captain Rosario," Zalcon said, "you have won
your share of contests. I'm afraid you never had a chance of
winning this one."

Zalcon's attempt at consoling Rosario had the opposite

effect as the Phantom sank deeper into the gloomy realization of his plight. Everything these space pirates said only served to intensify his apprehension that he was nothing more than the helpless pet of indifferent masters.

The Phantom's meager remnant of treasure was the only thing that stood in the way of the Maraudians' next and greatest conquest. Now that Rosario had surrendered his secret, the space pirates were all but ready to get under way. This type of cooperation was something the terrible Terran appreciated. In a fraction of the time that scanning would have taken, he had acquired what he needed to conclude this annoying detail in his new plan.

After Rosario had divulged the location of the treasure, Terran seemed to relax his calloused attitude toward his captives. In a more congenial tone, he said, "We still need your cooperation to help us understand exactly what the temporal disturbance involved."

Even though Rosario did not understand the concept of temporal disturbances, Terran offered no explanation. Instead, an atmosphere more friendly than hostile came over the officers of the *Maraudor*.

"As one pirate to another," Zalcon said, "we can appreciate you for the fierce opponents you are to your *peers*. That quality is one we each share in our separate worlds."

Rosario waited for Zalcon's words to settle before responding. "You call us pirates, and rightfully so," he said. "But we're no match for the likes of you. We know that now, to be sure!"

"If it's any comfort to you," Zalcon continued, "we took all of Lafitte's treasure, too." Bragging like this was as close as they would ever come to friendship. "It's our way to take everything of value wherever we strike. I know you feel the same, so you can appreciate the spirit in which I speak."

Rosario took advantage of this heartfelt moment to ask, "And you say you will return us to our ship?"

"Of couse," Zalcon said. "That is our agreement."

Under normal circumstances, Rosario could have easily detected the lack of sincerity in the space pirate's glib response. But now, desperate to believe what Zalcon was telling him, he was more than willing to cooperate in the frantic hope that the Maraudians would do what they promised.

The next part of the interrogation would involve a device that they called the Hat. Another piece of the miraculous technology stolen from the Illuminosity, this wondrous instrument would allow them to scan the Earthlings' subconscious minds and glean from them every detail of their experiences, even though the subjects might have no conscious recollection of the events.

The Phantom's compliance greatly reduced the strain on the equipment that was caused by the usual resistance from such meddling into every corner of the mind. This meant that Terran's team could move briskly on the medium-speed setting while maintaining the mental integrity of the subject. There were many questions that needed answers—unknowns that still stood in Terran's way of retrieving his fabulous fifteenth-century prize from the China Sea.

Rosario lay back on a couch covered with comfortable but unidentifiable hides. He was already wearing the Hat, which Mandoon had placed on his head. It resembled a hangman's hood, but without the front mask. Since Rosario had no waking knowledge of what they wanted from him, the process required nothing more than wearing the Hat. He felt a slight tingling sensation that induced drowsiness when the cerebral scanner was engaged.

Rosario closed his eyes as the mind reading began. Almost half of the session was taken up with finding that point in the sea of Rosario's subconscious images where the time spike had occurred. Holographic pictures appearing within a large transparent sphere in the middle of the room told Rosario's story.

Terran, Zalcon, Mandoon, and four technicians watched the tale unfold as they scrolled through, looking for clues and revelations. By the end of the session, all they had learned about the time spike was that the *Tortuga Diablo* had been shipwrecked on some island and the crew marooned.

As Rosario was being escorted back to his compartment, he passed Knox, who was being led to Mandoon's lab. Although the Phantom did not look any the worse, the boatswain was apprehensive.

"What's it like, Cap'n?" he asked.

In sharp contrast to the permanent grimace on Rosario's face, his tone was warm and reassuring. "It was easy," he said. "I almost fell asleep. No worries."

Rosario rested while Knox was tested identically. The

boatswain revealed little more, except that the environment where they had been shipwrecked was tropical and teaming with carnivores.

The scanning sessions were repeated every six hours. The second scans depicted the dangerous struggles for survival that Rosario and his men had been through. The pirates had been able to establish a small fortress only after many of their original crew had fallen from horrific encounters with the carnivores of the land, sea, and air.

There was a recurring scene of a volcano located in the central part of the jungle island. In each of several nocturnal occurrences, a crimson beam could be seen as it shot out endlessly to the stars from the center of the ominous cone.

A jolt of excitement flashed through the lab as the space pirates recognized what they were looking at.

"Could it be?" Mandoon said incredulously.

The Maraudians knew that only the Lamorians, also known as the Children of Eden or the Cradle Race, were capable of such technology. The Lamorians were the only people ever known to possess the fabulous Esseen Crystals. As legendary as the crystals themselves, the Lamorians were a part of the Maraudians' mythology. Little was known about their existence except that they came from a garden planet called Eden, and that the ancient hieroglyphs on Qwarz portrayed a crystal beam that shot out of a pyramid.

Legend had it that, every ten thousand years, a band of Lamorians would seek out a new sweet spot in the Universe, where conditions were right to start another Eden, another cradle for the human race. The Lamorians were the keepers of the miraculous Esseen Crystals. The most sought after treasure in the Universe, the gems had always been elusive, to the point that many believed they were only a myth. According to Maraudian legend, the astonishing crystals emanated a divine nurturing power that provided infinite wealth, longevity, and health.

Throughout all the peopled planets of Terran's galaxy, it was accepted as fact that there was never a time when man was not. On Qwarz, the cradle planet, there remained the ancient jade hieroglyphs, which told the undeniable story of the Lamorians' existence. Of all the worlds of the Qwarzian Galaxy, Qwarz was the birthplace of the human race. There, in the Valley of Siniah, the Lamorians created with their crystals a Garden of Eden that lasted ten thousand years. Eventually, however, the people became distanced from the Esseen Crystals and lost sight and understanding of their powers.

If the volcano's beam was truly what they thought it was, Terran's crew had made the discovery of the ages!

"How can this be?" Terran asked, perplexed.

"Somehow, this must be *their* time spike!" said Zalcon. His guess was as good as any. "What else *could* it be?" The first officer actually trembled as he dared to translate the possibilities: "If this is something of Lamorian origin, Captain, we may have found the spoor of unimaginable wealth, something so awesome that no amount of gold or treasure could compare to it."

The compartment seemed to pressurize with the magnitude

of the implications. Terran and the first mate felt giddy as they imagined the approaching tidal wave of wealth. It was the hope—or maybe fear—of all Maraudians that a day would come when they would encounter their own mythology firsthand.

"If indeed," said Terran, "we have stumbled upon the ancient race from Eden, then the possibility of actually possessing the Esseen Crystals may also exist."

The captain and his first officer were elated with this idea.

The third round of sessions with the Hat revealed the appearance of three new men from the future and their plan to escape the island. The sphere reenacted many battles with beasts in the day-to-day survival as the pirates and the newcomers wandered about, trying to escape.

The fourth round was winding down, yielding nothing new of interest, until the very last series of images appeared. These showed Rosario and four of his men, including Knox, sitting around a table with the people from the future. The oldest of these was showing Rosario and his men a picture.

Suddenly, one of Terran's team recognized the image in the picture.

"A Lamorian timeship!" he exclaimed. "A tabernacle for the fabulous Esseen Crystals!"

An astonished gasp swept through the science deck.

The future people were apparently a family—a father and his two sons—who claimed to be from the year 2006. The story that was unfolding in the sphere indicated that the future people knew where the Lamorian timeship was located.

Terran focused his team on analyzing all aspects of the images as they continued probing for every bit of memory that was attached to these future people.

By the end of Rosario's and Knox's fifth sessions, the Maraudians had confirmed that they were indeed on the trail of the most fabulous treasure of all time. The future people had seen it and knew where it was, but had no idea of what they had found or its significance.

Terran's former aspirations had melted away by now into irrelevancy, along with Cheng Lo and his sixty-two treasure ships in the China Sea. This new cataclysmic turn of events was all that mattered.

In the midst of the Maraudians' unprecedented enthusiasm, the buccaneers were left unattended in their quarters, which made them claustrophobic. They longed to escape, but rarely spoke about it. They didn't need to, for there was no doubt what they would do if the opportunity presented itself. Whenever they were not being interrogated, they had been confined to this room. Aside from receiving regular meals, they had nothing to do except contemplate their hopeless situation and sink deeper into a bottomless pit of depression.

The sessions with the Hat had seemed pointless. During each one, nothing was said to them. Afterward, they were returned to their quarters without a clue about what they were doing or what was wanted of them.

"How long is this gonna go on, Cap'n?" Knox asked wearily. "What do they want?"

Rosario had no answers for the frustrated boatswain. "What choice do we have," he asked, "whether it's one more sitting or a hundred? Unless you're tired of it all.... If so, we can try to cut Terran and some of the others down. Are you ready to go out with a flash?"

"Without so much as a cutlass between us?" Knox asked. "Not yet, Cap'n."

"Right," Rosario said, glaring at the boatswain. "Well, let me know if you ever change your mind. It won't take much more of this routine to change mine."

The Phantom felt absolutely helpless. Except for the short trips to the scanning room, it had been some time since he or Knox had seen the outside of their tiny cubicle.

Terran, oblivious to the needs of these men, whom he was treating like hothouse plants, left orders to Mandoon's crew to comb through the data for anything they might have missed. Then he went into a private meeting with Zalcon that lasted hours. When the two men emerged from the conference room, they had a plan to track down the Esseen Crystals. They would have one final session each with Rosario and Knox for the sake of being thorough, and then they would be off to find the future people.

"I'm sure you've given it some thought, Captain," Zalcon said. "What are we going to do with the Earthlings? We don't want to take the time to return them to the surface, do we?"

Zalcon had said it all. It was his place to voice the unpleasant options that lay in the preparations to get under way.

"When the time comes," Terran replied, "we'll do whatever is most efficient. Make ready for departure."

While Mandoon set and calibrated the time portal, Terran and the science crew pored over their information. They would go to San Francisco, a city in California, in the year 2006. But first they would implement their standard procedures while orbiting to learn what they needed about the culture and customs of the future people.

When they awoke, the two men of the *Tortuga Diablo* found Zalcon standing over them in their sealed compartment.

"Stand and face the hatch," he said calmly.

They followed his directions without question.

"We are about to go two hundred years ahead," Zalcon said.

Realizing that they were being dragged into another time odyssey, Rosario and Knox grimaced.

"Can't we be released before you undertake this next mission?" Rosario asked in desperation.

Zalcon shook his head apologetically. "There's no time for that now," he said. "We'll take you back to your ship when we return. The captain will explain everything." Before they could respond, Zalcon continued in a confident tone, "Of course, we now understand what it takes to travel the time tunnels without the risk of abrasion."

Knox turned to Zalcon to object.

But Zalcon snapped, "Here now, eyes front! Steady now, it'll be just another moment."

Suddenly, a blinding white lightning bolt exploded, brighter than the center of the sun, filling every molecule of vision, a flash that seemed endless, but in fact was instantaneous.

Aside from this signature effect, which they recognized from their last temporal jaunt, there was nothing to indicate any change in time to Rosario and Knox as the *Maraudor* now orbited the Earth in the year 2006.

Moments later, the hatch rolled open, and Terran appeared in the doorway.

"My apologies, gentlemen," he said. "I hope you can understand that, until I could be sure of what I was dealing with, I had no choice but to keep you confined to quarters. As you may still be of some service to us, I am obliged to keep you on board while we undertake this next part of our mission. However, so long as you in no way interfere with our operations, you are now permitted to move freely about the ship. I assure you, as soon as we are done, you will be returned to the *Tortuga Diablo*."

Rosario and Knox felt a surge of hope in these words.

"You say we are free to move about, Captain?" Rosario asked, wanting confirmation.

"That is correct."

With that, the captain and Zalcon left the compartment. Rosario and Knox watched them disappear around the corner as the hatch, which had always closed automatically, remained open.

At first, they were reluctant to leave the chamber, which they regarded as their prison cell. They stood immobilized, letting the thought sink in that their confinement had ended. There was the open door.

Knox looked nervously at his captain.

"What have we got to lose?" Rosario said. "We may never have a chance to see a ship like this again."

For the first time in this ordeal, Knox smiled. "Aye, Cap'n, let's 'ave a look about, and see what we can see."

Their lust for adventure lay like molten magma just below the surface, waiting to surge at a moment's notice. Before they knew it, they were lost, as they turned this way and that, making their way through the maze of the aft section. The passageways and compartments seemed to go on and on in all directions. Rosario could not imagine how big the ship actually was. Nor could he picture in his mind's eye what the *Maraudor* looked like when viewed from afar.

After a short while, they bumped into Lieutenant Zane.

"Out and about, I see," he greeted them warmly.

"Yes, sir," said Knox. "But although we're free to move about the ship, we dunno where anythin' is."

"I have a little time to show you around," said Zane. "I suggest we start with the galley."

Embracing their new sense of freedom, the Earthlings accepted Zane's cordial invitation. Since the galley was close by, they were there in an instant. Zane took them over to a huge box built into the bulkhead, which had two glass doors with runes beneath them and plates of food within.

"This one," he said, pointing to the door on the left, "is the *aubrice*, a cold stew concoction. And that one is the *catheequia*, also a cold selection, but without the gravy. I'd go with the *aubrice*, if I were you. That's *my* favorite. Food is always available here."

Recognizing the fare, Rosario was less than enthusiastic. "We'll come back if we get hungry," he said.

"I recommend that you take in the view from the spacewalk next," Zane said. As they made their way upward, he added, "What you are about to experience will seem like a walk across the ship's weather deck. Although you will think you are outside the ship, you will actually still be within its impregnable repel-lite hull."

Soon they were standing before a hatchway that looked as if it led to the exterior of the ship. To the left, there was an object on display.

"This is a miniature scale model of our ship, the *Maraudor*."

The two buccaneers were delighted with this revelation.

"She's a mighty strange-looking craft, I'll say that," was Rosario's only comment.

"It boggles the mind to think that this is what it takes to sail the sea of space," Knox marveled.

As the hatchway opened and they stepped out, the Earthlings found that, despite Zane's explanation, they were not ready for what they felt. Since neither of them had any idea of what outer space was really like, there was nothing to prove that they were not suddenly walking on the outside of the ship in the endless night. They had no way of knowing that if this were indeed the case, they would have been instantly suffocated, frozen solid, and floating free in space.

Although they had no concept of the reality of outer space, they were nonetheless mystified by the experience. In long moments of silent marvel, they took in the spectacular and enchanting vista. They were standing on top of a wide catwalk that was an exact holographic image of what would be their view of space. Behind them was the superstructure with the command bridge on top. In front of them, the catwalk extended one hundred yards before reentering the forward section. Four sky barges were connected to the long slender starship, two on each side, looking like shields on an ancient Viking longboat. A huge double-barreled sonic cannon turret was mounted on top of the forward section where the skywalk reentered the ship.

The initial impact of the view held the Earthlings spellbound. Even as Zane said goodbye, neither of them heard their guide take his leave, nor did they know that as soon as he was out of sight, he called Terran to make his report.

"I never knew this was 'ere," Knox uttered through his amazement. "Sure, I seen the stars before, but I 'ad no idea of the way things really are."

Knox was speaking his mind, hoping it would bring him to some new understanding of his place in all this.

Rosario was on the same tack. "If we survive this ordeal and make it back to the *Tortuga Diablo*," he said, "we'll be the only ones to have ever seen this view of the sea of space, as Terran calls it, where our own Earth spins in blue majesty beneath us."

As usual, progress was slow when the mother ship first arrived at a new planet—or in this case, a new century of the same planet. It took a while before the technology, languages, and all the rest began to make sense to the space pirates.

Far beneath the orbiting starship, there was now a myriad of satellites in close orbit. Terran was worried that they might detect the *Maraudor*, but it soon became evident that his ship was unnoticed.

As the Maraudians orbited in the silence of space, they diligently collected and analyzed their data to determine what was happening on the surface. Their focus was greatly enhanced when they discovered the global web of digital intelligence called the Internet. Finally, the first comprehensive report on all that was known about the ones they were calling the future people was ready for consideration.

While the buccaneers were discovering the *Maraudor* and her mysteries, the space pirates were analyzing and assimilating the data they had compiled from the Hat, so they could plan how to proceed.

"We know their names," Terran began, "their place of business, and their schedule. They are all of the same family, a father and two sons. They have had firsthand experience with the Lamorian timeship and have pictures to prove it. According to our information, they operate a combat simulation facility called Paintball Jungle. We also have maps of their facility and pictures of their faces. Information on them is readily available on the web of intelligence that now encompasses this treasure planet. If there are any other considerations we have not covered, now is the time. The first phase of this mission to obtain the ultimate prize is clear.... We must abduct the trio and bring them aboard the *Maraudor* for some sessions with the Hat."

A few moments of silence followed while some staff members conferred in low tones of agreement, but there was no more input.

Terran sat down as Zalcon stood to take over the meeting. "First of all," he said, "there is a problem with effecting a surface landing in this time period because of the net of tracking and spotting devices that encircle the planet. We will have to go back in time again, 1890 or so, in order to land undetected. This is where I want to go."

He pressed a small remote device, which made a blue screen light up on the wall.

"This is a map of an area just northeast of a city called San Francisco. We'll land here, where the Paintball Jungle backs up against the Napa River. As soon as we arrive, we'll use the time portal to take us the rest of the way into the future. With luck, we should remain undetected as we make our way into the Paintball Jungle. We'll pose as paintball players and play out the day until we get the opportunity to spirit the three away."

"The rough spot in your plan, Commander," said Terran, "is the unlikelihood of catching all three of them together at one opportune moment. Getting them away unnoticed among hundreds of players will also be thorny at best."

"Agreed, Captain," Zalcon said. "But a physical reconnaissance of the site should provide solutions to these unknown factors. The Jungle's videos on their website will give us a clear picture of the paintball sportsman's normal behavior, so we can fit right in."

"We will take this matter up again," said Terran, "after we all get some rest."

As the meeting ended, Zalcon took Terran aside and asked, "What shall we do with Rosario and Knox?"

Terran answered without hesitation. "We'll keep them around while this thing develops. We may still need them."

On the spacewalk, Knox's mood of enchantment changed to gloom as he thought of all his lost mates. "Things will never be the same again," he sighed.

With that, Rosario, too, was swept back into despair. The painful realization that their great brotherhood was all but extinct pierced the cosmic splendor. The memories of what they had been through, along with all they had lost, vaporized the rapture of their spacewalk with an intense resurgence of contempt for the terrible Terran that burned white hot in the hearts of both men.

"Maybe," said Rosario, "we could sign on with Terran…, go where he goes…, until we can repay him what he has coming."

The Phantom was trying on an idea he knew would never fit.

He and Knox continued walking, falling silent for some time as the fascination of space mesmerized them once again. Their thoughts changed back from the irreparable past to the fantastic potential of the future that was unfolding before them. The idea of Earth as just another one of countless planets, islands in the infinite cosmic sea, gave them a deep sense of mystery, which ignited their spirit of adventure as never before. Seeing this in their lifetimes gave them confidence when they realized they were on the greatest voyage of their lives.

Halfway down the long spacewalk, they were sufficiently accustomed to the cosmic vista to resume their conversation. They had been in denial, but now it was time to face what was all too obvious.

"Of course," Rosario said, "our biggest problem is staying alive after Terran no longer needs us."

Trying to come to grips with each new revelation in their ever-changing reality, Knox frowned as his captain's words smacked him into focus. "Aye, Cap'n, we can never trust 'im to deliver on anythin' 'e might say. Fact is, unless we can get back to the surface some'ow, we won't 'ave a chance of survivin' this ordeal. There's only two priorities, as I see it, Cap'n..., escape and sendin' 'im down under. I must confess, I'll take whichever comes first."

The Maraudians had various ways of assimilating

information. One of their more extreme methods was a pill, which provided a comprehensive, though temporary, grasp of large volumes of data and training. Used on rare occasions, the pill had no side effects. This mission was just the type of situation the pill was made for. Terran wasted no time implementing the method on his away team as they finished their in-depth briefing and focused on the scene at Paintball Jungle.

Mandoon declined the pill, even though he would go along to operate and guard the time portal. The members of the away party for this mission were Terran, Zalcon, Zane, Mandoon, and four others.

As Lieutenant Zane dispensed the magic pills, he said, "No worries. These are the next best thing to knowing what you're talking about."

Everyone laughed, but it was true. For the next seventy-two hours, they would have a thorough grasp of everything they had heard, studied, and practiced. Not only did they have replicated currency, but they recognized it and could easily calculate any transaction. Zalcon and two others had driver's licenses, knew every traffic regulation, and could drive a car, even though doing so was not in the plan. This degree of thoroughness was Commander Zalcon's signature touch.

After internalizing the extensive collection of Paintball Jungle videos, the crew left, confident in their ability to come across with authenticity. The year was 1890 as their sky barge approached the landing zone just after sunrise on a secluded bend, a few miles from the mouth of the Napa River.

FOREST FOX

Book 3

THE INHERITANCE
PIRATES OF MARAUDA TRILOGY